THAT WOMAN
FROM D'LO

THAT WOMAN
FROM D'LO

Robin Whitfield

To order additional copies of this book, contact:
Xlibris Corporation
1-888-795-4274
www.Xlibris.com
Orders@Xlibris.com
19989

My father, Clarence Nathan Whitfield, a handsome, sensitive man, adored by my mother, Della, was the strength that kept our family keenly aware there were others on this planet to deal with. That is the reason, this book is dedicated to them along with my wonderful wife, Myrtle.

CHAPTER ONE

Hilda came from an aristocratic southern family and had five brothers and no sisters. She was the youngest of the family and upon the death of her father, was much surprised to learn that he had willed his entire his fortune to her. Her Poppa, as she called him, ran a train from Clarksdale, Mississippi to Bogalusa, Louisiana and he was a southern gentleman who really knew how to make a nickel squeak. Of course, Hilda was never deprived of anything she needed or wanted. He told her, never get rid of the old family home when he died.

Her mother had long ago passed away, sometime during the beginning of the first World War when Poppa had property in the Delta around a little town named Isola. Poppa had several tenants on the farm land and he prospered very well acquiring a large house in D'Lo, a lumber town, on Highway 49 south of Jackson, the state capitol.

The large house had been the property of one of the administrators sent down from Pennsylvania to oversee the Finkbine Lumber Company in the middle 1900's, when the town of D'Lo was prosperous and well known for miles around.

Hilda lived in the old family home in D'Lo since her return from up North as most people around the area would say, which was Poppa's last wish. It seemed she always did what her Poppa asked of her. Some of Hilda's neighbors became leery about her comings and goings from the house since her secretive move back into the community. She was getting up in age and was not as careful about her appearance as she use to be. This caused much concern among her neighbors and close friends. When she came back to D'Lo from up North, as local people would say, she was still a great beauty and carried herself with much dignity. Her home, however, was badly in need of repair.

Hilda's best friend Ila came one day to check on her and found that the inside of the house looked as bad as the outside. Ila told her that she needed to get someone to help take care of the house and yard since Jerlene, the family housekeeper, had become suddenly ill and died. Hilda's mind seemed to wonder as she heard Ila chatting away, not knowing a word she was saying. Her mind was dwelling on the speculation among the blacks in the quarter that Jerlene had been poisoned or murdered in some subtle manner. Some rumored that voodoo had something to do with it, since Jerlene had been visited by several characters from the Chalmette area of New Orleans. This was the same area where her mother had lived before departing for the Mississippi Delta years ago. It was told that these visitors would stay with Jerlene at Hilda's old home when they were in D'Lo. Jerelene was given permission by Hilda long ago to stay on the premises until she came back to live in D'Lo. No investigation had been done since no one fully complained and no relatives showed up to claim the body. She had been living in the old home as a caretaker since Poppa died. It was what Hilda wanted and she had told Jerlene that she didn't know of anyone she could get. Her nieces and nephews were out of the question. They didn't even come around anymore since she quit giving them money and were left completely out of Poppa's will.

Finally, coming back to reality, Hilda said, "Ila, I am going to start being more careful with Poppa's money because it is going fast." Hilda wanted Ila to think that she didn't have much of Poppa's money left because if she really knew, she would tell her friends. Hilda chuckled a little, knowing full well that she had plenty of Poppa's money to last for a long time.

She smiled as she confided to Ila, "I may have to move into one of those elderly housing projects. I won't have any upkeep and maybe with my little Social Security check, it would be easier for me to live there. While living up East, I lived high on the hog, never missing any cotillion or entertainment function. Traveling to Europe and South France twice a year with the family who employed me as nanny for their daughter. Just think of all those clothes I had to buy for special occasions."

With a hint of a smile, Hilda watched as Ila would listen intently and shake her head as Hilda talked to her. Ila would leave Hilda's house and go by a couple of her old friends and tell them about poor old Hilda. Of course, Ila, now was getting elderly so they would take everything that she said with a grain of salt. As far as Hilda's health, it was good because she was able to get in her car and go places but never into Jackson proper, she would always say. Hilda was becoming very reclusive and even when Ila would come by, she was beginning to feel a distrust toward her.

One day while Ila was visiting, Hilda had some picture albums out on a table. Ila noticed that Hilda was very cautious and would not let her look at two or three of the albums and flatly told her that she could not look at them because they were special to her. During high school, Hilda had a boy friend that she thought had hung the moon. They were very close before Hilda became pregnant by her Poppa, and after the incident, she hardly talked about her boy friend.

It had happened the weekend that Poppa came home half stewed to the gills. Hilda had been abruptly awakened when Poppa crawled in bed with her. Poppa had always been a gentle person but she had never experienced what he forced her to do that night. No one in town knew of the incident and she and Poppa didn't talk about it even with her brothers. Later on, when Hilda approached Poppa about not feeling well and the doctor told her that she was pregnant, Poppa said he felt bad and hurt over the situation but abortion was out of the question. Due to nature, Hilda didn't have any ill feelings toward her Poppa because she felt that he in his drunken stupor, hadn't realized what he was doing.

After a long discussion, they decided that Hilda would go to an unwed mother's home in Natchez. They both decided that if any one questioned her absence, they would say she would be away visiting for about a year.

It was easy to make an excuse for a year, so upon her arrival back in D'Lo, she told everyone she had attended a private school for young ladies in Natchez. Having a child out of wedlock, especially incest, was something that was never talked about during the late thirties and early forties. Young ladies would never get themselves in this type of situation. Getting pregnant without being married was taboo. If it did happen, the girls were whisked off somewhere, like Natchez, New Orleans or South Carolina. Usually, they never came back with their babies, which was a sad thing. If the babies did return with the girls, they passed off as relatives. Hilda had never discussed her situation with anyone, not even Ila.

As her mind wondered back in time, a smile came to Hilda's face as she thought of the books that were off limits to her friend, Ila.

Her thoughts wondered back to her graduation at D'Lo High, then to Mississippi College, where all good Baptist girls were expected to attend. Her mind was full of the year she had spent at the unwed mothers' home in Natchez before Mississippi College.

Her mission now was to try and find who had adopted her baby girl and she had gone back to visit the home. She stayed at the Eola Hotel for one summer and posed as a volunteer worker at the home for unwed mothers. Seven years had passed since Hilda had become pregnant at the age of fifteen. All these years she wondered about her baby girl and had a desire to see her. Many nights she dreamed that she had seen her.

Upon arrival at the home, Hilda was accepted with open arms, not only for being incognito, but for the charitable donations she made with Poppa's money. She was praised for her work at the home and would not shirk any task that came her way. Hilda knew that one day she would be able to look through files and find the information that she wanted so desperately. For that reason, she would work anywhere she was needed.

One night she was asked if she could work in the evening. There were lots of babies at the home at this time and help was needed. She quickly told them that she could work anytime.

Hilda had one thing in mind and that was to find where the old files were stored. The night that she worked, she had lots of time by herself. She walked around every room in the house looking for possible file locations. Underneath a staircase on the second floor there were a number of boxes and on some you could see the word "files" written across one end. Of course, the writing was not very legible and she noticed up close that some had dates written on them. Her heart pounded, thinking that she might be close to finding her baby girl. There were too many workers around for her to start opening and looking at the boxes. Maybe, she could do it later before leaving for the hotel. She went back to the nursing station in the front of the house and noticed everyone was busy.

She sat down for awhile and her mind wondered back to her high school sweetheart, Anthony Leo. Would life been different if Anthony had been the father of her child? She loved him, she knew with her whole heart, but Poppa would not approve of him and she had to slip around to go out on dates with him. The main disapproval of Anthony by Poppa was that he had such a cocky attitude and was always bragging about his heritage in Pennsylvania. Anthony's grandfather did come from the old country, Poppa had told Hilda. They had migrated after World War 1 from Poland and started a bakery business in Pennsylvania. Everyone of the Leo children had gone through college, but not one had chosen the bakery business. Leo's father had chosen the business field and had gained an influential reputation in the world of administration. His family had moved to D'Lo from Pennsylvania during the great times of the Finkbine Lumber Company. Matter of fact, Finkbine Lumber Company had put D'Lo into the 19th century. Anthony's father was an administrator of the company. The Leo family had lots of adjusting to do moving from Lancaster, Pennsylvania to way down south in D'Lo, Mississippi. Of course, the first thing that was done before moving was building a big mansion near the plant on the only street running from the main highway. This was the street where most of the big homes had been located since D'Lo became prosperous. Many big homes were built in 1916 after the arrival of Finkbine. Who brought lots of new buildings to the little southern town. Three new hotels were in business, a bank was growing and so was the social life.

Poppa told Hilda she seemed to have changed. Little did he know, that it was because of Leo. They become great friends and slipped around to see each other when possible. But when the incident happened that weekend with Poppa, it was difficult for her to tell Leo that she would not be seeing him anymore which happened the day before she left for Natchez. She knew that if she stayed around D'Lo, Anthony would be blamed for her condition. She loved him too much for him to have to endure the gossip of a small town like D'Lo.

Suddenly, one of the nursery workers came by and said something to Hilda. Hilda took notice of how many workers were on duty for the evening. As some left for home, she began planning her strategy of getting into those files that she had found under the staircase. She went upstairs and looked around the area where the file boxes were stored. She got some dusting rags and a broom hoping that she looked as if she would be trying to clean up the area. She mentioned to the other workers before she left that she was going to do some cleaning upstairs, just in case she might be needed elsewhere. Hilda had checked to make sure that she was alone before moving the boxes around. She noticed that some of the boxes had dates on them. She immediately started searching for the year that she was at the home. Her heart was pounding as she moved the boxes from side to side, pretending to be dusting and sweeping. She almost fainted as she came upon the box that had the year she had been at the home. She was dizzy as she gazed at the date.

She had to sit for a minute to regain her composure. As she sat there wondering what was in the file box, the worker from the first floor came by looking at her and inquired, "Are you feeling alright? You look worn out, maybe you should go home and rest." Hilda was startled but she told the worker she was alright. As soon as the worker left, Hilda began dusting and cleaning again until the worker was completely out of sight. She nudged the box upon another box so she could raise the lid because the tape had long ago been broken. She was shaking as she went from one folder to another. The folders had been stapled and only a name was visible at the top of each.

The lighting was not very good to see by but she paused at each name. It was difficult for her to believe there were so many files in one box. She was beginning to get discouraged until she came upon a name that was difficult to read, but she made out the word D'Lo underneath it. Her inquisitive nature told her to open up the file. Even if it wasn't hers, she would find that maybe someone else had been here from D'Lo. Her hands were shaky and sweaty as she loosened the staples.

Inside the folder, she saw her name, "Hilda Lou Webber", in hand printed letters, underneath the caption "Mother of child". Reading further, she saw the printed caption, "Father of child", and the name, "Horace J. Webber". A shiver went over her body. It was a dark secret that would have been blamed upon her high school sweetheart, Anthony Leo. No one would ever know that her Poppa had come in one weekend from work, half drunk and overpowered her in bed. She knew that her Poppa was a wonderful man and she still loved him and couldn't believe it had eveer happened. When Hilda approached Poppa about being pregnant, he had told her she would have to go away for a year to have the baby.

Dizzily, Hilda read the document inside the file which was titled, "State Adoption". Her hands were numb and shaking. The first line read, "Name of Baby, "Gloria", which stood out like a neon light. Scanning on down the sheet, she saw the printed line which read, "Name of Adoptive Parents" and underneath were the names she had been hoping to find, "Mr. And Mrs. Jason Jackson Langley, 5400 Langley Place, Hartford, Connecticut".

Hilda broke down crying at the thought of not seeing her baby. She calmed herself and went to the front desk to let them know she would be going home for a rest. As she left, she pondered the scratched writing of the name and address that she had put on a small piece of paper pulled from the side of one of the file boxes. She said to herself, "At least I have the name and address of my baby's adoptive parents. I will sleep on it and tomorrow I will send word for Poppa to come and get me."

Feeling somewhat relieved the next day, she tried to conjure up some way to visit Hartford. Since she had finished college, maybe she could find a nursing or nanny position there. Of course, she would have to convince Poppa that she wanted to find employment in New York City because if she told him Hartford, Connecticut", he would ask, "Why Hartford?" Hilda was sure Poppa knew all the information contained in the file folder.

Poppa picked Hilda up the next morning and was very quiet while driving home. Hilda said, "Poppa, have you been feeling well?" He blurted out, "Why did you want to come home on such a sudden notice?" Hilda said, "Poppa, I am tired and need some rest before I look for further employment. Aren't you glad to see me?" He quickly replied, "You know I am glad to see you and have missed you, but I worry about you. I worry about you being left alone when I die. You need to think about getting married so someone can take care of you when I am not here". Hilda put in her plug she had been waiting for, "Poppa, when I get rested, can I go to New York City to find employment? Who knows, I might find me one of those Yankee boys to take care of your baby girl". She looked at him as he smiled from ear to ear saying, "Baby, whatever you want to do is fine with Poppa. Just be sure you know what you're doing because I don't want you to go through another episode like you experienced with Poppa. Poppa is so sorry for what he did to you and will have to bear that guilt for the rest of his life. I hope that you will still love Poppa and remember that he loves you dearly. You know you are Poppa's baby. Whatever happens to you or wherever you may go, when Poppa dies you will be taken care of. All that I ask, "Don't dispose of the family home because Poppa will leave money to take care of you and the big house. The boys are able to take care of themselves, but I worry about you."

Hilda said, "Poppa, I am going to rest around the house for a month while I get myself prepared for my visit to New York City. In the meantime, I will contact Lenora, a girl friend of mine from Jackson, who is now living in the big city. She invited me to visit her several months ago. I will see if I can visit her with thought of seeking employment". Poppa nodded, saying, "Poppa will set up a checking account for you before you leave because it might be awhile before you find the type of employment that you wont. Poppa will miss you so much because the boys seldom come around now since they are busy with their own families."

Hilda knew that he was right about her brothers. He had financed all of the boys in some type of business but they were too busy to take up much time with her and Poppa. Some of her brothers had married girls Poppa had not approved of, but he never complained about it. Poppa missed Momma so much and he would take short trips either to New Orleans or Memphis. Hilda felt that he had gone off to find him a woman. Of course, it seemed perfectly reasonable with Hilda, since he was only in his middle fifties and still a handsome man.

Hilda noticed his happy expression as they arrived at the house in D'Lo. It was wonderful coming home after being in Natchez for several months and she was tired of housework.

After parking the car, Poppa and Hilda started into the house when Poppa's maid, Jerlene came out to greet them. Jerlene had been with Hilda since the day she was born. Matter of fact, Jerlene had delivered because her mother was unable to get to the local hospital in time. Sometimes Jerlene would discuss this with Hilda, saying she was in a hurry to get into this world. Both of them would laugh about it. Hilda had a wonderful rapport with Jerlene. Hilda always felt that Jerlene was appreciative of her family.

Poppa had accumulated information about Jerlene and her mother when he had a farm in the Delta.

Jerlene was the offspring of a woman called "Queen Arabella", who had migrated with her baby to the Mississippi Delta from the voodoo dens of the New Orleans French quarter. Her white father had been an administrator with the city of Chalmette. Her mother had been threatened when she became pregnant with Jerlene, so she got a ride with some people coming to Mississippi to work in the cotton fields. Jerlene stood out among the dark blacks of the Delta because of her creole skin. Most of them tolerated her, but after her mother died she didn't seem to get along very well with the other blacks. Poppa saw how Jerlene was being treated by the other blacks, so one day he asked her if she would like to move into his household to work. She did at age 15 and was accepted by the family. Her bedroom was just down the hallway from Hilda's bedroom. When Hilda's mother died, Jerlene actually took over the responsibilites of running the house. Jerlene was now 40 and Hilda was approaching 25 and Hilda still depended upon her for suggestions. Jerlene was always there for her when she needed to talk.

Going up on the veranda that encircled the Webber house, Jerlene walked arm in arm with Hilda. Poppa smiled to himself, thinking maybe Hilda would settle down for awhile since she was at home. Maybe she would forget about going to New York city.

Jerlene giggled, "Miss Hilda, I fixed everything you like to eat for supper since Mr. Webber told me you were coming home today."

Hilda said, "I am so tired of housework I could just croak and especially the same old food they served at the home where I did volunteer work. I know you have been taking good care of my Poppa because he looks good." Jerlene's face lit up like a spark had gone off in her soul and left for the kitchen, giggling out of control.

Hilda looked toward Poppa and his face was red as a beet. The look on his face confused Hilda but she left saying she was going to lay down for a bit before supper. On the way to her bedroom, Hilda noticed how well kept the house looked. As she lay down across her bed, she thought, "I don't have to worry about Poppa, Jerlene will take care of him for me."

Hilda slept for about an hour, and, upon waking, she just lay there for awhile. She could hear voices but couldn't tell what direction they seemed to be coming from. She eased upon the side of the bed, listening, until she decided that she would seek out those voices. As she moved out of her bedroom into the hall, she moved quietly until she heard voices coming from Jerlene's bedroom. The door to her bedroom was closed but she could hear the voices more audibly.

She heard Jerlene say, "Now Mr. Webber, you are going to have to watch yourself since Miss Hilda has come home. She might not like the relationship you and I have. I would not want to hurt her feelings. She is such a sweet girl and I feel she would not approve of you being in my bed."

Mr. Webber replied, "Jerlene, you know I love my daughter, but you and I have had a good relationship for years, ever since you started working for me. You know that a man often needs a woman and I would be lost without your company at times. Hilda wants me to let her seek employment in New York city and I agreed to that, but honestly, I will be worried to death over the situation. Jerlene you are almost like a wife to me. You and Hilda are going to drive me crazy."

Hilda was frozen in her tracks as she heard them talking. She didn't budge as she leaned against the wall in the hallway. Again she heard Jerlene say, "Mr. Webber, because you took me in when I was desperate for help and my own people had turned against me because I looked more white than black, I will do anything you ask me. Your family has always treated me with kindness and you taught me how to talk and think. Once you told me that if I really wanted to, I could go to a big city and pass myself off as white. Those things have made me appreciate your family and I will be with you as long as I am needed."

Mr. Webber said, "You better go see about supper. Hilda will be getting up soon."

By now Hilda's head was swirling with confusion and as she came to her senses, she almost fell against the opposite side of the hallway. As Jerlene came out of her bedroom, she heard the back door of her bedroom close which meant Mr. Webber had gone out the back way. Hilda smiled as she saw Jerlene walking toward the kitchen.

Jerlene came up to Hilda, "Baby, I am glad that you are home. You need to rest awhile before you decide what you want to do. Your Poppa tells me you want to go to New York city. You go on up to the parlor and sit awhile and I will have supper for you and Poppa in a little while." Hilda smiled as she heard Jerlene say, "Poppa", as she walked toward the parlor. She flung her shoes off as she entered the parlor and curled upon the stuffed sofa.

Sitting there, her mind was going in every direction it seems. So many questions which needed answers. How many years had Poppa and Jerlene been close? Do they sleep together when no one else is here? Do my brothers know about them? Did my brothers have sexual affairs with Jerlene before they married? Hilda thought to herself, "I am not supposed to worry about anything cause Poppa said so. I can not criticize my father because he is looking after my welfare. I am supposed to rest and be prepared because tomorrow is in my future. Who knows what will take place when I get to New York city? I hope one day to see my baby girl Gloria and I will as God is my witness."

Hilda didn't wake up until she felt Jerlene shaking her shoulders, saying "I hope you are more rested since you had a good nap. Miss Hilda, I hope you are plenty hungry because I went all out tonight, you being away so long. I felt you needed a good meal. I don't know why you have been looking so puny these last few months, but it seems to agree with you. You look so pretty, Miss Hilda. When you were growing up, I thought you were going to be so ugly and I envied your good looks even back then. If you go to New York, you need to get good and rested. I need to look at your wardrobe to make sure you are up on all those new styles that they're wearing up East. I want you to knock all those yankee boys off their feet, cause about time that you found yourself a fine, rich husband. I know they are there, all you have to do is shake the bushes."

Hilda was taking all this conversation in with a smile as big as a Cheshire cat. She slapped Jerlene on the behind as she passed by, saying, "Jerlene, you are full of it today, girl. If you know so much why haven't you found yourself a man? There are lots of men around D'Lo who would love to have you, especially those of your color and probably some of the darker ones. Jerlene, you know what I mean. There are lots of light colored people in the D'Lo community and you know what that means."

Jerlene said, "Miss Hilda, come on out and say it, "White men have been in the black folks' beds. I agree with you because I have black friends that are more light skinned than me and I know who their fathers are. Matter of fact, they have asked me to go out with them, but I think it's trashy going out with just anybody and all they want is my body. I have to care about a person first. They are the pillars of this little community but I will never tell because I don't want anyone to find my body floating in Strong River or Dabbs Creek. And, the colored men that want to go out with me just want to get in my pants. I saw what a hard time my mother had raising me, and I don't intend to copy her. My father was supposed to take care of me and my mother, but he couldn't keep us a secret. When his folks found out about him and my mother, they disinherited him and he had to go to work. My pregnant mother had to run for her life because she had been threatened several times. She was a voodoo queen making a good living in the French Quarter of New Orleans, but one day she was told to leave after being beaten unmercifully. She had friends that hitched a ride for her to the Mississippi Delta and that was where I was born. My mother lasted only a few years and she died of a broken heart on my twelfth birthday. A month before my birthday, she told me everything, just as I'm telling you now. It was hell for me because every man that saw me wanted to screw me. I was so glad when Mr. Webber took me in. I will always be indebted to that man. As far as I am concerned, he can do no wrong. You and your Poppa have always treated me like I was one of the family. I wouldn't have anything if it wasn't for you all. What would I do and where would I go if it wasn't for Mr. Webber? I am gonna stay right here and take care of him while you are gone to New York I know you will be back one of these days and tell me all about everything you saw and did. That's the glorious day I am looking forward to. You'll probably come driving up in a big old car with a handsome man sitting beside you. I will love you for it. Miss Hilda, I want the best for you because you're a good woman with a genteel nature."

Hilda sat up straight on the sofa and said, "Jerlene, what I want you to do is take care of my Poppa because I can tell that he doesn't seem to have as much energy lately as he used to have. If he gets too sick to write me, I will be expecting you to keep in touch with me. I want you to promise me that right now on this stack of bibles." Jerlene looked over at Hilda and there were several bibles on a table near the couch. Hilda had them in a stack before she knew it and clutching Jerlene's hand, she said, "Jerlene promise me you will do what I asked you to do."

Jerlene started crying, "Miss Hilda, I will, I promise you anything. Just don't go off and stay too long. Remember, Miss Hilda, if something happens to Mr. Webber, what am I gonna do?" The expression in Jerlene's face was disturbing to Hilda. She had never thought of what would become of Jerlene if Poppa should die. Of course, as long as Jerlene lived she would have her with her.

She immediately said to Jerlene, "Don't you worry. If Poppa goes, you will always be with me. If I am not here in D'Lo, I will send for you wherever I am."

Jerlene's face lit up like a torch. She said, "Miss Hilda, would you really do that." Hilda said with a giggle, "I say what I mean. You ought to know that by now. You don't think I would throw you out so all those hot blooded blacks in the quarter could get their hands on you. I have noticed several times when going to the post office with you how those tall black studs look at you with a smile and rub their big, bony hands across their crotch." Hilda got so tickled that she fell backwards on the couch, saying, "Jerlene, you have nothing to worry your mulatto head about. Also, I want you to go with me shopping in Jackson next week. Jerlene said, "Miss Hilda, you want me to go shopping with you! What are your friends in D'Lo going to say? I can just hear it now, "Miss Hilda Webber and her colored maid went shopping together in the big city". I don't want you to get talked about on my account." Hilda said, "You let me worry about what might be said. Really, I don't give a country damn about what some of these old prudes in D'Lo might say. I could really give them something to talk about, if they knew some of their men were seen in the quarter after dark. Also, some tried to start the rumor that Poppa had come by his money cheating and mistreating the share croppers on the small plantation he had near Isola, Mississippi. But, that was years ago after the depression, so I will not worry about that now. I have other important things to think about at this time."

Hilda got up from the couch and walked toward the front of the house and looked into the darkness. Turning around toward her bedroom, she noticed Jerlene had left her presence. Before getting into bed., Hilda opened all the windows and slipped into bed with the cool, night, air blowing through her bedroom. She thought, "I really hate to leave this sanctuary, yet I have got to get out and try my wings. If things don't work out for me then I can always come back here. I will never give up this house because Poppa has asked me to never, never give it up. If push comes to shove, and if I can't come home and take care of the house when Poppa dies, then I will let Jerlene do it until I get ready to come home permanently."

Hilda finally went to sleep and was awakened by Jerlene saying, "Miss Hilda, it is almost nine. Do you want some breakfast now?" Slowly coming to her senses after resting so peacefully through the night, she said, "Jerlene, is today Friday? If it is, let's go into Jackson and spend some of Poppa's money. Poppa will carry us and then he can visit with some of his old friends at the capitol while we shop a spell. I could drive but it is not too lady like to be seen driving a car, especially southern girls. You fix me some grits, toast and some of that dark coffee. I sure hope that you have some of that sculpenon jelly left that I like. Leave it to me, I will talk to Poppa just as soon as I get something decent to wear on my body." Jerlene jumped up and clapped her hands just as if she was sweet sixteen again. Almost crying, Jerlene said, "Oh, Miss Hilda, I am surely going to miss you when you leave for the big city." Jerlene left for the kitchen and as soon as Hilda finished dressing, she went to the big living room in the back of the house where Poppa could always be found when at home. Hilda approached Poppa, saying, "Poppa, would you drive me and Jerlene into Jackson this morning? I would like to purchase a few items before I leave next week for New York. Don't you think that you could visit with some of your old friends at the capitol for awhile until we could do a little shopping? When we get through you could take me to the Mary Frances Tea Room for lunch. Jerlene would be glad to go to the Krystal on Capitol Street while we enjoy our lunch together."

CHAPTER TWO

Poppa jumped up from the big recliner as if doing a jig, saying, "Hilda, sometime you have the best idea of spending the day. I have been wanting to go to Jackson for a month, so now is just as good as any time to go." He winked at her, saying, "I know you'll want a little cash. Just tell me how much and I'll run to the bank and get us some for the day."

Instead of saying how much money she might need, she said, "Poppa, can I just charge it and let you pay later. It is difficult to say how much I will truly need." Smiling Poppa said, "Baby girl, whatever you want to do is alright with Poppa. Get Jerlene something that she needs because she does her best to take care of you and me and that big old house."

Hilda said, "Poppa, I am going to miss you and Jerlene when I go to New York City." As Poppa got up to leave for the bank, Hilda put her arms around his neck, crying like a spoiled child. Poppa said, "Let me go and get us some money to spend." Hilda moved toward the front of the house calling Jerlene. Jerlene finally heard her calling and came in from the front lawn. As Jerlene came into the house, she said, "Miss Hilda, did you call me?" Hilda said quickly, "Get you glad rags on, Poppa will be back in a short while and we'll be on our way to Jackson. You do want to go with me?"

Jerlene looked so happy and as she jigged around holding her skirt above her knees, she sang, "Oh do da day." Hilda looked at Jerlene, noticing how good the years had been to her, because she was still a good looking woman. As Jerlene pranced into her room, she was still singing.

Within an hour, they were off to Jackson and as they drove down Capitol Street, Poppa said, "I will let you two off at the Vogue and will pick you up in about two hours at the same spot."

Hilda said, "Poppa, you are the best, so you go and have a good chat with your friends."

As Hilda and Jerlene went from shop to shop, people would stare at them, especially at Jerlene. Hilda every now and then would stare back at them. Jerlene whispered to Hilda, "See what I meant about me being with you. They looked at me like I was some fool and I heard someone saying, "Look at that black girl with that white lady. She must think she is somebody having her own maid following her around.

But you know something, I don't care, as long as you are here with me. Miss Hilda, I have really enjoyed getting out of D'Lo for awhile and seeing how the other folks live. Looking at some of these people today, I feel that I am very fortunate to have you and Mr. Webber. I know when you leave that I will have to stay close by the house because Mr. Webber seems to be feeling poorly these days. It maybe just because you are leaving us for awhile. Well, anyway, I will look after him the best I can."

Hilda said, "Jerlene, Poppa should be by in a short while, so we had better get back to the Vogue. I don't want to keep him waiting in all this traffic. I have never before seen so many cars and people on Capitol Street. Jerlene followed along until they were at the Vogue. Poppa had just pulled up at the curb. He seemed to be very happy, humming a tune, as he opened the doors for them to get in.

He said to Jerlene, "Here's some money for your lunch because you told me that you wanted to eat at the Krystal on Capitol Street. While you do that, I will take Hilda to the Mary Frances Tea Room for lunch, just up the street a block."

Poppa pulled up to the curb in front of the Mary Frances Tea Room and as Jerlene got out, she said, "I will be back shortly and thanks, Mr. Webber, for lunch." Hilda noticed Jerlene as she blended in with the other people walking on the street. Hilda said to herself, "If Jerlene wanted to she could easily pass over the color line."

Poppa noticed Hilda watching Jerlene as she walked down the street and he chuckled, saying, "She could easily get lost among all those white folks and she sure looks better than some of them."

Hilda snipped back at Poppa, "You were thinking just what I was thinking. I am so lucky that I have Jerlene to look after you when I am gone. It seems I can trust her more than any of my five brothers. Peculiar, that we have not had a visit from any of them since I came home."

Entering the Mary Franes Tea Room, several people from Simpson County, acquaintances of the Webbers said, "Hello." Two ladies were inquiring about where Hilda had been since they had not seen her in several months. Hilda told them she had been visiting relatives in Natchez and was planning a visit to New York soon. One lady blinked her eyes at Poppa and smiled very affectionately. Poppa told Hilda that he knew that she worked in the Governor's office and had seen her there when he visited a friend at the Capitol.

Hilda enjoyed lunch with Poppa and as they left the tea room, they noticed that Jerlene was outside standing by the car waiting for them. She was all smiles as she was joined by Poppa and Hilda. She immediately said, "Mr. Webber, this has been a fine day for me, being with you and Miss Hilda." Hilda looked at Poppa and smiled.

The ride home was quiet until Poppa drove into the driveway. As Jerlene opened the car door, she said, "What do you all want for dinner tonight? Just name it and I will fix it." Poppa laughed out loud and said, "Right at this moment, I am not hungry but check with me later in the afternoon." Jerlene pranced toward the porch and into the house, leaving Poppa and Hilda talking out in the yard.

Hilda walked toward the yard swing and as she sat down, she said, "Poppa, come here and talk with me awhile." Poppa gazed down at the ground as he sat down beside her. He knew in his heart what Hilda was about to say to him. There was a moment of silence as he gazed around the huge yard where he had worked many hours trying to make it look just the way Hilda had wanted it to look. Actually, he was proud of his handiwork because it looked like a picture from a southern magazine.

He turned his head toward Hilda and she immediately said, "Poppa, I am going to miss you and Jerlene when I leave next week for New York. My tickets came in the mail yesterday from the railroad company and next Wednesday, you will have to take me to Meridian to catch the train. I will only have one change and this is in DC. Lenora will meet me at Grand Central Station in New York city on Friday morning at ten. I am planning to stay with her until I can acquire my own apartment. She has now been living in New York for almost two years and seems to be doing well as a librarian for the city schools, so she writes. She really aspired to be an actress but as yet she has not been able to do any acting except in some off Broadway plays. She was really good in the college plays and such a beautiful voice. She still hopes for a career in the theatre. I will immediately start looking for employment upon arrival and will keep in touch with you and Jerlene."

Poppa felt that it was time for him to cut the strings and let his baby bird fly away to find her way into the real world. He reached over and hugged Hilda with a bear hug, saying, "Baby girl, your Poppa will always be right here for you whenever he is needed. As soon as you get settled, let me know and I will have the bank wire some money to whatever bank you desire. Being in New York, you are going to need some cash for awhile. I hope you are happy doing whatever you wish but remember that you can always come home.

Jerlene came from the house into the yard humming a tune. As Jerlene approached, they arose from the swing and Poppa said, "Jerlene, fix us some country fried steaks and hot biscuits for supper. Hilda smiled because she knew that was one of Poppa's favorite foods, hot biscuits. Poppa excused himself and left for the back yard and Hilda slowly moved into the big house. Hilda laid down for awhile and was dozing when she heard someone in the back yard. She left the front parlor and strolled to the back porch and as she gazed out into the yard, she saw a young man of about fifteen years of age talking with Poppa. Hilda noticed that he had black features but his skin was lighter than Jerlene's. In the kitchen,

Jerlene was also staring into the back yard with much interest as her mind flashed back to the time she was pregnant with Cicero. She was uneasy but she knew that one day her son, Cicero, fathered by Mr. Webber, would come face to face with his real father.

Jerlene wondered what Miss Hilda would think her Poppa having a baby by her colored maid. When she was pregnant with Cicero, she had a difficult time keeping it a secret from Hilda. Near the time when she thought the baby would be due, she told Mr. Webber and Hilda that she might be going to New Orleans to visit some old friends for a couple of weeks. This was fine with them and Hilda told her that she was going on a trip with some friends from school and might be gone for several weeks. Jerlene said that she would get Katie Mae, her friend from the quarter to look out for Mr. Webber while she was gone.

With Hilda on her trip and Jerlene feeling poorly each day, she told Mr. Webber that she would be back in a couple of weeks. Mr. Webber thought Jerlene had left for New Orleans but actually she was at Katie Mae's house across the railroad tracks in D"Lo having her baby. Katie Mae went to the Webber house each day to fix meals and see about things, Jerlene would tell her what to do. After about a week, Jerlene returned to the Webber home, leaving her baby with Katie Mae to raise. Jerlene would see the baby often because Katie Mae was her good friend. She was someone Jerlene could go to and talk her heart out. Mr. Webber was glad to see Jerlene and told her Hilda was coming home within a few days.

On the day that Hilda was to arrive, Mr. Webber said, "Jerlene, are you feeling well? Did you over do yourself while visiting in New Orleans? I think you should rest awhile every day so you will be feeling better." Jerlene smiled at Mr. Webber, saying, "I'll be alright since I am back home."

Katie Mae was always willing to listen, because she, too, had mixed blood flowing through her veins. She knew what it was to come from a half-breed family. Katie Mae said to Jerlene one day, "That baby boy is going to be a killer. There will be some more white negroes in D'Lo in the not too distant future." Cicero started looking at girls by the time he was twelve and called himself heavy dating by his sixteenth birthday. He was a very handsome black boy with the features of a white boy.

Hilda had left the back porch hideaway and as she came into the kitchen, Jerlene was jolted back to reality, being caught unaware of her being nearby. Hilda said, "Jerlene, who is that nice looking young man in the back yard with Poppa?" Jerlene stammered for a moment saying, "That's my friend, Katie Mae's son." Hilda quipped back, "He certainly looks like part of your family,. Really, you and that boy favor a lot. Where has he been that I've never seen him before." Jerlene said nonchalantly, "Oh, he's been around D'Lo for some time. Go ahead and call Mr. Webber that supper is ready? Don't want those biscuits to get too cold."

Hilda started to the back yard to get Poppa, when the young man who was talking with Poppa approached her. Cicero said, "You must be Miss Hilda, Mr. Webber's daughter." Hilda looked at him with a smile saying, "Yes, I am Hilda, Mr. Webber's daughter." Hilda noticed his handsome features and how he carried himself. He said, "I have heard so much about you and hoped that I would be honored to meet you one day. Katie Mae, my Mom, told me what a nice person you are and Jerlene loves you just like you were her child."

Hilda didn't really know what to say to him. He seemed like a nice young man. Hilda said, "Your Mom is Katie Mae and what is your father's name?" Cicero seemed upset as he said, "Really, I don't remember my father and was told he died from an accident the year I was born. But Katie Mae, my Mom, has raised me, along with Miss Jerlene's help. Miss Jerlene has been mighty good to me, it seems all of my life, as I remember. She is always giving me some new clothes and spending money for school. She visits us very often, really, she seems just like an aunt." Hilda smiled very beguiling as her mind began to wonder back and forth through certain situations that had happened. In her heart, she knew this young man was really her half brother. He looked so much like Poppa and if he was any whiter, it wouldn't be difficult for anyone to see the resemblance. His square jaws like Poppa's, his eyes, the spitting image of Jerlene's, made him a handsome young man.

Hilda wondered what she should do, but as usual, she said to herself, "I'll worry about that another time." She bid Cicero, "Goodbye" as he left smiling. He waved his hand, saying, "See you again soon, Miss Hilda. Enjoyed talking with you. I had heard that you were a beautiful lady and now I know for sure." Waving her hand at Cicero, she climbed the steps of the back veranda and sat down. Thinking to herself, "Should I muddy the water, causing hard feelings between her and Jerlene, or her and Poppa?

Since I am preparing to leave next week for New York, maybe it would be better if I just let things rock as they are so everyone will be in a good humor. I feel that Jerlene thinks I know that Cicero is her son by my Poppa. Supper was a quiet affair, only Poppa mentioning that his little girl would be leaving for the big city on Monday. Hilda looked at Poppa and wondered if he knew she thought Cicero was his real son.

Everything was great just like it was, she thought, "I am not going to do or say anything to change it for now." Hilda said, "Poppa have you taken care of my bank draft for the New York bank? If you have, "Thanks, Poppa, because I know you don't want your little girl to be stranded way up yonder without any means to survive. I am not really worried about anything else since my good friend, Lenora is settled into the New York society, so she says. Her last note said she had much to tell me and we were going to have a ball when I arrive. I do know she was very popular at Blue Mountain College and went on several soirees to Europe while in school.

Laughing out loud, she said, "Jerlene, I do hope that she is not too fast for me to keep up with."

Jerlene put her hand quickly to her face, snickering, "Miss Hilda, you'll just have to watch out and be the southern lady you are. Us southern women are different from the ones up North. Mr. Webber and me want you to come back here with a fine looking man one of these days. Miss Hilda, I am counting on it. Mr. Webber, "Don't you feel just like I do?"

Poppa looked at Hilda, blinking his watery eyes, almost tears running down his face, saying, "Jerlene, all I want for my baby girl is to be happy."

Tuesday evening before leaving for New York on Wednesday was a busy day for Hilda. Jerlene had planned a huge dinner with all the trimmings. Hilda was so enthralled in packing clothes and discussing with Jerlene her complete wardrobe. In so doing, she had discovered many dresses that she gave to Jerlene and Jerlene pranced around the house from room to room singing and dancing. Jerlene knew that there was a sadness to this whole situation and this was her way of trying to make everyone feel better. Hilda knew the strategy behind Jerlene's behavior. This made her feel more at ease about leaving Poppa for Jerlene to see about. Dinner had been served around five and by ten, all three were exhausted.

Everyone had a glass of port and Hilda said, "Poppa, we need to retire so you will feel good driving me to Meridian to catch the train."

Poppa looked over at Jerlene and then fixed his eyes on Hilda, saying, "This place will be sad tomorrow night as you are riding toward New York."

Hilda said, "I will be back at Christmas time and it is only three months away. Now you know Poppa, I am going to miss you and Jerlene so much. I might be back just any time. I really don't know what's ahead for me in the big city. If things don't work out for me relative to a good position, then I will plan otherwise and return home to my Poppa."

Mr. Webber stood up and started toward his bedroom and as he passed Hilda he threw both arms around her and Hilda noticed his cheeks were wet as he pressed them upon her face. Mr. Webber made a glancing look toward Jerlene as he continued moving toward the hallway leading to his bedroom.

Hilda got up and immediately hugged Jerlene goodnight, saying, "I need to rest awhile in the morning so I want be getting up until around ten, which will give him ample time to get ready and be in Meridian, as the train leaves at 2 PM. Jerlene, I am so excited about this whole adventure. As you know, it will be a positive adventure for me. I must know if I will be able to survive on my own terms in life, I can't always be dependent upon Poppa. Of course, if it was left to Poppa, he would have me depending on him financially for the rest of my life and not wanting me to budge no further from D'Lo than Jackson. I know he would shower me with all the things I need but yet I would never know if I could every fly alone in this world."

As Hilda closed the door to her room and flopped down in an oversized chair, left by her mother, she felt a slight chill run down her backbone. She laughed to herself thinking, that rabbit really ran over my grave. She got up quickly getting dressed for bed. She wasn't sleepy but tired and as she tried to relax, her baby came to her mind.

She thought to herself, will I ever be able to do what I want to do, so I can be able to see my baby once again. She said, "Dog gone it, I am really going to try. I know I want be staying very long in New York or at least I feel that way now."

CHAPTER THREE

By morning, Hilda was tired fighting to get some sleep. As she lay in bed, she thought I will just have to sleep on the train. A knock on her door around ten by Jerlene was her clue to hit the floor running.

As she put on her robe, she heard Jerlene saying, "Let's hurry and not let those biscuits and grits get cold. Your Poppa is up there waiting for you."

Hilda thought to herself, "Am I doing the right thing leaving Poppa?" As she approached Poppa at the dining table on the back veranda, a fear of loneliness swept over her. This was almost like someone saying to her, "Have you really thought about what you might encounter in the next few weeks or months. You will not have anyone to talk with or discuss situations that might arise. Remember you don't want Poppa to know what you are really planning to do relative to your baby, Gloria."

Poppa looked over at her as she sat down. Hilda looked straight into his eyes and immediately Poppa said, "Baby girl, you look so tired, don't you want to wait a day or two before you leave?"

Hilda said, "Poppa, we have already postponed this trip once because I was supposed to have left last Monday and here it is Wednesday. I will be fine once I'm settled on the train."

As they finished breakfast, Jerlene sat down beside them for coffee. She said, "Miss Hilda, do you have everything organized in your purse that you will need. I know you have your bags packed right because you and me fixed that last night before you retired." She handed a piece of paper to Jerlene saying, "This is my address in New York, with telephone number where Poppa or you can contact me for now. I don't know how long I will be there, but I will notify Poppa when I change locations. If I get a good position then I might want an apartment by myself. Both of you pray that things will be good for me until I see you again."

Mr. Webber got up and walked toward the front of the house saying, "If we are going to make the train, we must be on our way. I have already loaded your bags in the car." Jerlene quickly wrapped her arms around Hilda, crying and tried to talk but couldn't. Hilda gave her a big hug and said, "You will hear from me in a few days. Just take care of Poppa for me." Hilda rushed toward the car looking back at the big old house, in her mind, she wondered, "Will I ever see this place again?"

Not a thing was said until they approached Highway 80 from Highway 49. Poppa looking out the sides of the car from left to right said, "One of these days all the trees you see around will not be here much longer and some interstate highways will be coming through here. You will get to see the change but I want be here."

Hilda knew Poppa was trying to amuse her and she loved him for it. He had always been a loving Poppa even though that one incident happened. Poppa had suffered a heap because of the guilt he carried around with him, Hilda thought. Probably any other daughter would have called the law and caused lots of trouble for their father but I just couldn't cause my Poppa to be ridiculed and shamed by others. He has told me many times that he was sorry for his actions.

Poppa drove the car into the Meridian railroad station at 1:30 PM and a porter came to remove the bags into the train station to be checked. Within twenty minutes the train chugged into the station. Hilda hugged Poppa and proceeded up the stairs into the pullman car. Poppa stood outside until the train started moving, waving at the window where Hilda had been seated. As the train left, Poppa could be seen in the distance still waving.

Gazing at her Poppa until she could see him no more, she wondered, "Would I ever see him alive again?"

On the train ride, Hilda thought to herself as to what she would have to do to accomplish moving on up to Hartford, sometime within the next few months. I will just lay that aside for now and think about it tomorrow.

First, I have to get prepared mentally to meet Lenora Packer, girl friend from Mississippi College, who has secured a pretty good job as a fashion reporter with a magazine. In this position, she had met lots of important people, celebrities and loved the fast lane which her job provided. Hilda felt like she could stand the pressure but wondered would she be able to compete in any way with Lenora.

Lenora was a model in her own right and had beautiful clothes to wear. Of course, she was not able to make any judgments until she came face to face with her friend. Lenora had insisted on her coming to New York and staying with her until she could get settled in a position.

During these days, places of employment, such as secretaries, bookkeepers, or maids, were just about the limit for women. Hilda had prepared herself to be a teacher and she was hoping to find a position in that field or a nanny to some child of wealthy parents.

As Hilda's thoughts clogged her brain, she dozed off and was awaken the next morning around 9: AM by a porter announcing, "Grand Central Station, New York city." Hilda pulled herself together after returning from the bathroom. She applied some make-up while gazing out the train window.

She saw Lenora standing outside looking at every person that disembarked from the train steps. When Hilda finally approached the door opening to get off, she screamed at Lenora. Lenora waved so prim and proper, rushing into Hilda's outstretched arms. Both were sobbing like two fretful children.

Lenora said, "Hilda, you are such a beautiful woman. I suppose all those buttermilk and sweet potato packs have been good for your complexion. The places I go are so smoke filled these days. I know that must be bad for your skin. I tried to take up smoking but I haven't learned to really care about it. I know you haven't tried smoking yet, have you?"

Hilda was shocked to hear her say such a statement. Hilda thought for a moment and came back quickly holding her nose upward in a sassy fashion saying, "Well, you know us southern girls, if we take a notion to try something, we do it." Hilda and

Lenora screamed at each other, laughing so much that people standing around seemed to become amused at them.

Lenora started waving her hands, motioning toward the entrance of Grand Central Station, saying, "My friend is out there waiting to carry us to my apartment. As soon as the porter retrieves your bags and get them outside to the limo, we'll go home for a bit of refreshments. Lord knows, I need a martini or a manhattan. Of course, here in New York, it is "Happy Hour Time" but down South it is time for a mint julep or ice tea. Girl, you are going to love this crazy town. Believe me, I have learned to love just about any type personality from a cultured, Smith College nymphomaniac to a withered, jaded fag. All in due course, you will find out what I mean when you meet some of my best friends. Honey, the fashion world is so interesting with a bunch of screwed up people but we get along so well together."

As Lenora and Hilda followed the porter to the parking area outside the station, Hilda could see a man waving his hand, motioning for them to come over to where he had parked. The man immediately got out of the limo and ran over to assist them.

Lenora started waving her hands, motioning to Hilda, saying, "Hilda, this is my best friend, Zack.

Zack looked at Hilda very curiously, then his gaze swept toward Lenora, saying, "From what you said, I was expecting an older woman. She looks younger than you."

Lenora said, "Zack always says the nicest things, especially if I don't completely agree with him on everything. We were talking seriously before you arrived about how some women make themselves look older because they really don't know how to use cosmetics to their advantage. We did agree on one item though and that was, it did help most women to some degree. I told him that you really didn't use much make-up, especially as much as I do. He said that a little is much better than too much. Of course, I agree you do look younger than me. You haven't been on this New York treadmill like I have for the past three years."

Hilda got in the back seat of the limo, still laughing at Lenora but making no comments. As they drove to Lenora's apartment,

Hilda noticed the streets as they rode along. Everything seemed so busy outside and her mind drifted back to the world from which she left only yesterday. In a way she was already feeling the pangs of being away from the small town of D'Lo. It was getting late in the evening and dusk was beginning to turn into darkness. It seemed just like a sea of neon lights were blinking directly at her. Hilda sat quietly as Zack and Lenora were talking about something that had happened during the day.

Zack slowed the limo down and then pulled into a parking area underneath a huge building. Zack got out and opened the door for Hilda and Lenora. Zack got her luggage and Hilda followed behind them to an elevator nearby. Going up on the elevator, Hilda noticed Lenora staring at Zack as if wanting to say something.

The apartment was on the 14th floor and as they left the elevator, Hilda heard voices. Lenora and Zack walked about twenty or thirty feet up the hallway to a double door which immediately opened up as Lenora knocked. As the door opened, there were several people milling about, shouting at Hilda, "Welcome to the Big Apple."

Hilda was overwhelmed and started hugging everyone. Lenora introduced Hilda, telling them she was her best friend from Mississippi. As the party wore on, Hilda looked around at everyone, she said to herself, "I am in a new world and if these people are Lenora's friends, then I must accept them, so be it."

Hilda noticed two women dressed like men, holding hands and every now and then would peck or kiss each other. In one corner were five good looking guys just talking but they seemed to move very loosely, accentuating what was being discussed with limp wrists and thrown back heads.

Lenora came over to Hilda, saying, "I know you are weary, so I am going to bring this party to a close."

Hilda smiled at Lenora and immediately Lenora started ushering everyone toward the door. Lenora showed Hilda to her bedroom, commenting, "I do hope you are comfortable here until you decide what you want to do. You know you are welcome and I am glad to assist you in anyway that I can. My work schedule is erratic and sometimes I may be out of the city for a spell but here are your keys, so you can go and come as you please. Tomorrow, I will be here so we can talk more. Get a good night's sleep."

Hilda didn't even unpack her luggage. She found in her small bag a gown which she put on and went straight to bed. Lying in the dark, her mind wondered what Poppa and Jerlene were doing. She finally went to sleep, as she whispered to herself, "I miss them already."

Hilda woke up but didn't hear a stir from anyone. She decided she would dress casual and as she was about ready to leave her bedroom, there was a knock on her door. As she opened the door, there was Lenora handing her a glass of juice. Smilingly, Hilda took the juice as she proceeded out of the bedroom.

In awe, Hilda observed the layout of the apartment with interest. Drinking her juice, she walked around looking and then noticed the beautiful patio on one side of the apartment. Hilda thought, this must cost a lot of money to rent a penthouse apartment of this caliber. Then she wondered, "Lenora must make a good salary." I want to pay my share of the expenses until I move to a place of my own. I will discuss that with her today."

Hilda walked out on the patio and Lenora came later with two cups of coffee. The scenery was beautiful from the penthouse. The sun was shining and the air was crisp. As they sat there looking, Hilda said, "Lenora, I want to pay my own expenses for staying with you because Poppa prepared for this situation. So, I want you to give me a figure as to what my expense will be and I will give you a check now. I don't know how long it will take for me to find a position. But, after I do, I will be finding myself an apartment. I will stick around New York for awhile but if I don't find something suitable for me, then, I may try Boston or Hartford."

Lenora's eyes looked at Hilda with surprise, especially after her mentioning Boston or Hartford. Lenora said, "Hilda no one is using that bedroom, so you stay as long as you like but the food is another problem. If you want to eat in, you will have to buy your food because usually my meals are on the go with work. I will let you know when I will be away, just be careful and enjoy yourself.

I really hope you will find a position in New York that you will like. Really, what kind of position do you prefer?'

Hilda immediately said, "You know that I have been trained as a teacher, which would be fine, maybe a "Nanny" to some very rich kid." Both of them giggled a bit. Hilda chimed in saying, "Really, a traveling "Nanny" would be my ideal position. This would give me a chance to see the world. I would have to find the right family for this position. Of course, I have seen a couple of ads in the paper for these types of positions. I will check with employment agencies and the ads to see."

Lenora said, "I wish you the best of luck. But, today I will take you to your first Broadway play, "Westside Story." It is a musical and the tickets were given to me by one of my fashion house clients. It is great to have the week-end off for a change."

Hilda remarked, "I know the musical would be fantastic and a great way to begin my life in New York, but Lenora you seem to be so tired, so why don't we just spend some time here in the apartment today?"

Lenora was quick to reply, saying, "Oh, know I must see this play and the company that gave me the tickets will have someone there, I am sure. These fashion houses are full of prima donnas and it is such a gossip machine. These artistic people seem to be hurt easily and they might be offended if I don't show up. Anyway, there might be some that you might want to know. Really, they are a good bunch but different. Several have helped me along the way since I have been in New York. We'll just relax for awhile and then we'll discuss what we plan to wear at the matinee. We must just knock their eyeballs out of their sockets."

After lounging around for a couple of hours, looking at fashion magazines, every now and then Lenora would make comments about fashion companies that she dealt with. As Lenora made conversation, Hilda felt that she was the same self-centered Lenora she knew at college. Her actions caused people to dislike her but she had several friends of the same degree. Even though they were not close at school, Hilda always wondered why she kept in touch with her. Hilda looking up from a chaise lounge, noticed that Lenora was no where to be seen. Walking inside the apartment from the patio, she heard noise coming from the kitchen area. She started calling, "Lenora, Lenora and from a small room, which looked like a pantry, came a voice saying, "I'm in here looking for ingredients to prepare a snack for us before we begin to think about what we shall wear to the theatre." Hilda said, "Don't bother, I will take you out for a treat or whatever, just name it. I don't feel like cooking just yet and neither do you. Isn't there some place or club near the theatre that we can visit before the play?" "Yes, there is the Tavern on the Green nearby where we can obtain an after lunch snack or a cocktail before the matinee," chimed Lenora. "Since we have plenty of time before dressing, get an hour's shuteye, that's what I am going to do," said Hilda. Lenora left for the bathroom and Hilda went to her assigned room, where she dumped everything on the floor and fell across the bed.

Hilda's mind was completely in shambles only dozing in and out of sleep. She was beginning to face the reality that she was in New York city and not in the town of D'Lo. Being homesick was beginning to emerge and she felt insecure. Thoughts whizzed through her mind, if she could really find a position, things would be better for her. The main thing was to keep busy and she vowed to herself tomorrow she would be out searching for a job.

As she lay there, Lenora knocked on her bedroom door and said, "We have about two hours before the matinee, so we need to get dressed and down to the tavern. You can buy me a cocktail, I really don't need anything to eat."

Motioning to Lenora in the affirmative, Hilda thought to herself, "Maybe she drinks too much. But, of course, I am not going to say anything about it just yet." Lenora sort of grinned and said, "I will call my favorite taxi when we get ready. He brings me home many times when I attend these soirees at different fashion houses. Sometimes I am a little bit inebriated from all those cocktails shoved in my face. He is rather cute but still acts like a gentleman, even when he brings me all the way up to my apartment.

Within thirty minutes, Lenora was on the phone calling her taxi friend and within ten minutes he was at the door. Lenora introduced Hilda to Rogerio and they were on their way. Hilda and Lenora sat in the back seat of the taxi and as they rode along, Hilda felt that Rogerio was staring at her in the front mirror. Hilda gazed a couple of times into the mirror and his eyes pierced hers as they met. They were at the Tavern on the Green within seven or eight minutes and as they left the taxi, Rogerio said to Lenora, "What time do you want me to pick you up at the theatre?" Lenora looked flabbergasted and stammered, "I will just have to call your number, ok." Saying not a word, Rogerio bounced off the curb into his taxi, waving as he drove off.

Hilda treated herself to a salad and sandwich while Lenora had her cocktails. Actually, she had about three and seemed to be feeling a little shaky as they left the tavern to walk a couple of blocks to the theatre. As they walked along, Hilda noticed that she was a little wobbly. Upon entering the theatre lobby, Lenora was trying to find a place to sit after handing the tickets to the ticket girl. They got situated inside the theatre and didn't move even during intermission. Lenora had several friends to come by as they recognized her, probably from some party they all had attended. Some of them were quite far out, especially their attire, thought Hilda. She had a rush of insecurity thinking about some of Lenora's friends, hoping they would not call at the apartment while Lenora was away.

When the play was over, it took a spell to get back to the lobby, as it seemed to be "Standing Room Only." Hilda looked around for Lenora, but Lenora was nowhere to be found. She had not said a word to Hilda about going to call her taxi friend, so she just stood there where she could be seen when Lenora returned. It wasn't very long before Lenora came back saying, "I had to call my taxi buddy and he will be here shortly. He has had one busy night." Hilda smiled at Lenora and she seemed pleased. Many thoughts about Lenora went through Hilda's mind as she stood waiting for Lenora's taxi friend. She seemed very friendly with him or at least it appeared that way to Hilda. Rogerio finally showed up complaining how busy the night had been and was very apologetic for being so long. Hilda and Lenora got in the back seat and within fifteen minutes they were back at the apartment. Upon arrival, Rogerio immediately said to Lenora, "Can I stop by for just long enough for something to drink? I know it is getting late but I haven't stopped for the last two hours or so." Lenora looked over at me and I chimed in, saying, "I am very tired and will be on my way to the bedroom. You all can visit as this has been a long day for me. Thanks for the wonderful evening and nice meeting you, Rogerio."

As Hilda closed the door to her bedroom, she immediately started preparing for bed. Within thirty minutes, Hilda was in bed with a million thoughts going through her head. As she lay thinking, it seemed to her that she could hear mumbles but not very audible noises coming from the living room where she had left Lenora and Rogerio. She looked at her watch on the night stand. It showed that she had been in bed at least two hours and there were still lights showing under her doorway from the living room.

She finally drifted off to sleep and woke up around ten. Throwing her robe around her, she immediately went into the living room and out on the patio. She observed Lenora holding her coffee cup, gazing out into space. Hilda stood, gazing at her, she seemed to look so worn out this morning. Hilda interrupted her stance by saying, "Good morning, and how are you?" Lenora turned her head toward Hilda, saying, "I have felt better but this morning, it seems to me that it has been years since I left my home in Mississippi for this jungle I am in now. I wonder why did I ever leave my happy home for this. I know I shouldn't be talking to you this way. I don't want to make you feel unwelcome or homesick. I suppose that I am just unhappy today. We need to plan the rest of the day, probably take a stroll through Central Park. There are really lots of interesting things to do and see here in New York City. Things will be falling into place when you secure employment and meet new people." Hilda gazed at Lenora as she looked out upon the city wondering if she really understood her. Definitely, she didn't want to become involved with her surroundings as Lenora was or as it seemed. Was she really involved with Rogerio and if so why be so secretive about it.

Anyway, Hilda retorted, "Whatever you would like to do today will be fine because tomorrow I will be out searching for me a nanny job. Somewhere in this big city there is a family who needs me to look after their child."

CHAPTER FOUR

Lenora looked at Hilda with a look of surprise saying, "Don't you want to just visit as a tourist before you jump into the world of employment. It is quite a different world than what you have been accustomed. I know it will be different for you than it was for me because when I arrived in the big apple, I was almost broke but I did have a position. I met some nice people at the fashion center and everyone was very helpful, especially for the first three months. After I got to know everyone, it seemed that some of them just drifted away and now I don't see some of them socially. Most of them, usually spend their off time in Greenwich Village, where most of the literati people live. If they are not there then they are at the theatre or gone to Provincetown for the week-end. It takes money for all these excursions and I spend mine on clothes because I have to look chic at my job. That's enough from me, let's get some casual clothes on and go to the Tavern on the Green for brunch. We might just meet some interesting people there. I'll call my taxi friend and see if he'll come running after I let him stay around for awhile last night. I hope we didn't disturb you with our shenanigans and it was late when he left."

Hilda said, "Lenora, this is your apartment and I am grateful to be here for awhile, so don't change your mode of living for me. I think brunch will be great and it will be fun just being outside on the streets looking around, so I am with you.

Lenora and Hilda proceeded to get themselves attired for their soiree at the Tavern. The Tavern was a great meeting place, especially for out-of-towners who had migrated to the big apple to look for fame and fortune. Lenora had met Rogerio, her taxi friend who parked on the street outside of the Tavern, three years ago. Lenora was penny pinching at the time because she was new to the city and her new job. Her taxi friend, Rogerio, helped her out by running her around the city and bringing food to her apartment, spending time with her. They got to know each other very well or at least Hilda thought so after last evening.

As they sat on the sofa waiting for Rogerio to arrive, Hilda said, "There's one thing about your friend, no one can say he's ugly. He is one of the most handsome Spanish guys I have ever seen. Of course coming from Mississippi, I haven't seen a lot. Did you say that he came to New York to attend college?" Lenora almost interrupted her but stopped abruptly saying, "Yes, he attended college for a short while but his grades fell short of passing because he was spending too much time working part-time. He says he plans to start back but I doubt if he ever will since he has done quite well as a taxi driver. He now owns three taxis in his fleet which are on duty night and day. That is the reason, he claims, that he can wait on me when I call. He would love to have me at his beck and call but I have it the other way around, he's at my beck and call." A smirk of a smile came across Lenora's face as she looked at Hilda, wondering what she would say after answering her question. Hilda smiled at Lenora, not saying a word, but in Hilda's mind she now knew what was going on within the apartment.

A sharp knock three times on Lenora's door brought her and Hilda to their feet. Opening the door, Rogerio greeted both women saying, "What do we have planned for the day? I know Lenora wants to show you around the city."

In a mildly rude tone, Lenora said, "We would like for you to drop us off at the Tavern and then after brunch, I will call you as to what we plan to do later."

Rogerio didn't look too happy with what Lenora said, but he said, "It will be my pleasure to do as you request."

Not a word was spoken all the way to the Tavern and as Rogerio pulled up in front for Hilda and Lenora to disembark, he got out of the taxi and hastened around to open the back seat door for them. Lenora said to Rogerio, "I'll call you later if that is ok with you."

He immediately said, 'Of course, it will be fine and you both enjoy the brunch."

Arriving at their table, Hilda noticed several people were waving and saying hello to Lenora as they settled themselves. While eating several people came by their table to converse with Lenora upon leaving. This brought some very strange ideas into Hilda's naive mind. It seemed that the men were more cordial than the women who stopped by for a brief visit.

Lenora commented very casually, "You can see that I have met a few people the short three years I have been in the big city. Hilda smiled and said, "The food is very good." Back in Hilda's mind she was hoping for the day she could be in Hartford trying to see her baby girl in some way. Deep in her heart she knew that this day would come to pass.

After about two hours, Lenora seemed to be getting nervous or at least that was the way it appeared to Hilda.

Hilda said, "I am ready to go or whatever you have in mind for us to do as you mentioned earlier about going some other place. If you want to we can go home and I could get prepared to go out to the employment agency that I called on Friday. They told me to come in Monday around 9: AM.

Lenora looked surprised and mentioned that she was tired, saying, "I will go to the phone and call Rogerio. He should be here within minutes."

On the way to the phone, Hilda noticed that Lenora was stopped by a gentleman and they talked for awhile. Upon his leaving, Hilda could hear him say, "It has been awhile and I want to call you soon." He took something from his pocket and put it in her hand as he left.

This really got Hilda's mind working. She couldn't see exactly what it was the gentleman put in her hand but it looked like folded money. Anyway, looking at the doorway of the Tavern where Lenora was now standing, in walked Rogerio. Hilda got up and proceeded toward the front and as she approached Lenora and Rogerio, Lenora said, "Let's just take a long ride up Fifth Avenue and around Forty-Second Street area on the way back to the apartment." Rogerio quipped, "Great, ladies as you wish."

Hardly a word was spoken as they drove up Fifth Avenue toward Forty-Second Street. Hilda noticed that Lenora kept eyeing Rogerio in the front mirror and the curl of a smile around his mouth as he looked up at the mirror often.

Hilda said, "When we get to the apartment, I need to do some errands this afternoon to prepare for my appointment on Monday."

Lenora looked at her in dismay saying, "You are really anxious to start working and I am sure that you will find just what you are looking for."

Hilda answered in a very optimistic manner, "Yes, indeed, there is a position out there for me somewhere."

Hilda looked around the streets as she settled back in the taxi and after leaving Forty Second Street area, she wondered about the contrast of how the areas differ from block to block. The Forty Second Street area was very crowded and noisy whereas the Fifth Avenue area with its chic shops was less noisy.

Arriving back at the apartment, Hilda quickly said to Lenora, "I enjoyed the brunch and will see you and Rogerio later. I have some things to pick up before Monday." She went outside to take advantage of the beautiful day and started walking.

It was a good day to walk and, so many thoughts came into her head. She wondered, if a position became available, would she have to relocate or what was really in store for her. She had been in New York for a whole week and it was time either to act or go home to Poppa. Before she knew it, she had walked several blocks, so she stopped at a small park near the street and sat down.

After sitting a while, she noticed it was close to 4: p.m., so she decided to walk back to the apartment. I will stop at a drug store and pick up something on the way, she thought, just to let Lenora see that I did go shopping.

Upon arriving back at the apartment, Hilda noticed that Rogerio's taxi was still parked as it had been when she left. She approached the door to the apartment, but it was locked, so she used the key that Lenora had given her. Opening the door, she went through the living room and noticed that the door to Lenora's bedroom was closed but she could hear audible voices every now and then. She entered the bedroom she had been using, and closed the door, but could still hear voices and laughter every now and then. No one had heard her come in from the street.

It was obvious to Hilda that Lenora was having some type of an affair with Rogerio. This whole week she had been in New York, Lenora was either gone or had company after Hilda had retired. She remembered that several times during the week, she had been awakened by noises coming from the living room or Lenora's bedroom.

These situations made Hilda want an apartment of her own, but first she wanted to find a place of employment. If she didn't find a position she was going back home to Poppa. Anyway, she felt homesick already. Another thing that bothered Hilda was that Lenora had never told her specifically where she was employed. When asked, she said her boss sent her on modeling or fashion assignments. She seemed to have everything that she desired, nice high rise apartment, and many clothes. But the aura around Lenora never seemed to be a happy one even when they were together. Some of Lrnora's friends who had stopped by the apartment seemed a little on the freaky side but were stylishly dressed. All of them seemed to have wealth and drove fancy cars.

Before retiring to bed, Hilda went out on the patio, hoping that Lenora would emerge from her bedroom, but this never happened. So Hilda went to bed, still hearing noises every now and then from Lenora's bedroom.

Monday morning, after leaving a note for Lenora, Hilda was up and gone before her friend emerged from her bedroom.

In the middle of the day when Lenora did come out from her bedroom, she said she wasn't feeling very well because she felt that she had neglected Hilda over the week-end. Yet, in her heart, she felt that Hilda knew just enough to surmise about her life in New York. After all, when she arrived three years ago in New York, it wasn't easy to find a position, as Hilda refers to a job. I had to take care of myself the best way that I could and that was, use my body if the occasion arose. Well, the occasion arose, probably too many times because after all this time still doing what I did the second month that I ran out of funds living in this big city. She still had men showering her with money just for an overnight stay with her or with them in their fancy penthouses. One such man that she had met on a soiree into New Jersey one week-end, had paid for a full year's rent on the apartment and was still giving her funds otherwise. But, it was ironic, since Hilda's arrival, she has been getting up pretending that she was going to her work when really there was no set location for her to be working. She would meet one of her freaky friends for breakfast because some of them did have a job. In her heart, she knew that this situation would have to end in some manner. She had not actually had a full time job since arriving in New York and the thought of doing this was not one of her greatest desires.

Hilda had a busy day as she had contacted three employment agencies. Matter of fact, it seemed to be her day, as she had been offered some positions that she felt good about. Two of those positions would mean that she would have to relocate if she accepted either one. She left her interviewer with great hopes of making a decision within the next couple of days. She would have to call Poppa as soon as she made up her mind on what to do. She had to make a decision because she was not liking her stay with Lenora as she felt that she was a bother to her private life. Hilda had no idea that Lenora was such a social butterfly. In Mississippi, she never showed these types of inclinations. Anyway, she would tell Lenora all about her good day when she arrived home.

Hilda arrived home at dusk because she treated herself with dinner at the Tavern. Upon seeing Lenora, she noticed the tired expression on her face. Many thoughts went through Hilda's mind but she greeted her with a hug, saying, "Girl, I may have hit pay dirt, as they say back in Mississippi. I was offered three jobs but only two of them were interesting to me. Both of them, I would have to relocate. Really, the one that stands out most in my mind is the Nanny job to a four year old girl for a couple that is going to

Europe and they want a Nanny to care for their daughter on their month's visit. I would go along on the trip, all expenses paid, plus salary. This couple will be visiting friends while in Europe.

Lenora doesn't this sound exciting?" Hilda was noticing how wide eyed Lenora had become and both were giggling and talking at the same time.

Lenora said, "Yes, it does but I don't want you to leave New York. We haven't been able to do much together and see this big old city. But you said that you had another position, now what is it all about.

Hilda stunned, looking into Lenora's tear stained eyes, said, "Lenora, are you happy here in New York. Sometimes you seem to be and other times you seem be unhappy. Tell me if something is making you unhappy. You seem to have everything a girl could want, a good job, nice apartment and so many friends."

Lenora quickly answered, "Shucks, forget about me, tell me about your other position."

"Nervously, Hilda began, "Well, let me recoup for a minute. The other position will depend on how well I perform the position that I just told you about. This couple that is going to Europe on an extended visit have some friends, that have a five year old adopted child, who wants a full-time, live in Nanny. They live in Connecticut. It seems all of these people are wealthy or at least that is what I was told at the agency. So you can see why I am so nervous talking about these jobs. I have to make a decision within the next two days."

Still wide eyed, Lenora just stared at Hilda, saying, "This could be the end of a short visit if you have to leave this quick but I understand and I don't blame you one iota. You have to look out for yourself and that is what I have tried to do since arriving in New York. I probably have not made good decisions but when I arrived I didn't have a great deal of money so some of my friends have helped me out of the hole a few times. I suppose I should try to find me a better way of making a living than letting someone else pay the bills. Anyway, I will worry about that tomorrow. After you make your decision, we'll have Rogerio take us out on the town before you set sail."

Many thoughts regarding Rogerio went through Hilda's mind but she was not in a position to judge the situation with him and Lenora. The air between them was not the same at different occasions when they were together. She didn't feel that Lenora was completely happy with the relationship but then she could be obligated to him in some manner. Who knows he maybe helping her in a financial way. Hilda was not at ease thinking about the affair.

Getting up from the couch, Hilda said, "Just as soon as I meet with this couple, who are coming down from Boston Wednesday, AM to talk with me about the position, I'll let you know. Really, I think this would be a neat position at least for a month. The trip in itself will be worth the trouble. Maybe at that time I will find out more information about the other job from this couple. I really need to get settled in a position so I want have to bother Poppa about sending more money to the bank. Anyway, I promised him that I would find a position. Of course, I could go home and he would support me and let me do as I please."

Deep down the desire to see her baby girl was getting more intense. Of course, Lenora didn't know anything about her baby and she would never tell her. She thought that Hilda was doing a lot of volunteer work at the unwed mothers' home in Natchez.

CHAPTER FIVE

All of a sudden Lenora said, "Well, we'll begin celebrating by going back to the Tavern for dinner tonight. Rogerio is coming by anyway and we'll have him to take us there and I will call him when we are ready to come back to the apartment." Lenora staring at Hilda commented, "Don't say no, if you do I will be disappointed."

Hilda was stunned about the dinner invitation and said, "Lenora, really I am tired after this run today at the employment agencies. So let's wait until after I find out about my position, maybe, we'll have something to celebrate."

Lenora's mood swung to the opposite side it seemed to Hilda. She got up from the couch, saying as she proceeded to the bathroom, "Ok, if that's the way you want it." Hilda waited for her return but Lenora stayed there, so Hilda went to her bedroom to prepare for bed. In her bedroom, Hilda listened to see if Lenora would return and in so doing fell asleep.

Hilda slept late the next morning because she knew that the next day, Wednesday, she would have to be on the ball for an interview with the couple coming down from Boston. In her heart, she was hoping that this would be the beginning of a new life for her and that someday she would be able in some way to see her baby girl. Her baby, Gloria, would be almost five years old and just the right age to be cute and loveable. Probably, she could have already been in kindergarten. She had tried to picture in her mind how she would look but she knew that she would be a beautiful child. She had a pang of regret not being able to see her all these years but by some hook or crook, she was going to be able to see her baby girl. She decided that she would stay around the apartment and get her wardrobe ready for the appointment next day. The door to Lenora's bedroom was closed so mid-way the morning she decided that she would see if she was at home. Opening the door, no Lenora was to be found and her bedroom looked as if it had just been cleaned up. Hilda thought maybe she went out to run an errand or spent the night with a friend.

Late in the afternoon. Hilda went out on the patio of the apartment to sit for awhile. Sitting there, she dozed off but was awakened by lots of laughing coming into the apartment. In walked Lenora with two women friends which she immediately introduced to Hilda. Hilda noticed that these women looked older, tired and worn than Lenora. All three, as noticed by Hilda, seemed to have had too much to drink. At times all three would be talking at the same time and she couldn't keep from laughing. Between chit chat Hilda could make out that they had been at the Tavern on the Green.

It was getting dusk dark and Lenora's friends were still visiting. Hilda felt maybe she should excuse herself and retire for the night because of her early appointment at the employment agency in the morning.

Getting up from her chair, she told Lenora that she enjoyed the company but tomorrow was going to be an important day, so she was going to retire for the night. All the women hugged her and said they hoped to visit with her again sometime soon. As she left, she glimpsed at Lenora's sad expression on her face. She really looked as if she wanted to cry.

Hilda immediately said, "Lenora, I hope to see you sometime tomorrow afternoon with some good news."

Moving toward the door to her bedroom, Hilda smiled at Lenora. Getting ready for bed, so many thoughts ran through Hilda's head concerning her prospective interview that was scheduled in the morning. She went through some of her papers that she had brought from home, hoping they would be of some help in the interview process. Finally, lying in bed, thinking of Poppa and Jerlene, she fell asleep.

Noise woke Hilda the next morning and she was glad that it did because when she looked at her clock on the dresser, it was time to rise and shine. She bounced out of bed and into the bathroom. She wore some of her most conservative clothing that was in her wardrobe. She commented to herself, "Well they want think that I don't know how to dress especially being a "Nanny." As she walked out of her room, she passed by Lenora's bedroom door and out the front on the way to her appointment. She was glad that there would be no confrontations of any kind before her interview. On the way, she stopped at a small café and had some breakfast. What she really would have liked was a cup of Jerlene's coffee which in her mind, she could almost smell it all the way from Mississippi.

She arrived at the employment agency about thirty minutes before her interview and seated herself in a comfortable manner to relax and meditate for a bit. The receptionist was scanning everyone in the seating area and as she noticed Hilda, she said, "Are you Miss Webber?" Hilda replied, "Yes, and I have an appointment at ten." The receptionist said, "Miss Webber, the couple to interview you have already arrived and would like to see you now." Hilda smiled and said, "I am ready." The receptionist said, "Would you please follow me."

Hilda thought to herself, I must make a good impression because Poppa would be glad if I found me a good position. As she followed the receptionist into the interview area, she cast her eyes upon a couple that seemed to be in their late thirties or early forties. In her mind, she immediately liked them and as she sat down a feeling came over her that made her think that this was the beginning of a new adventure.

As the receptionist introduced her to Mr. and Mrs. Jack Tate, she felt that she had seen them before. They were very cordial and said, "Miss Webber sit down here beside us and let us talk about the position we have to offer."

Hilda retorted, "Please call me Hilda." Mr. and Mrs. Tate smiled and said ok, "Hilda." Mrs. Tate said, "Hilda, we plan to go to Europe, touring several countries and we have a five year old daughter who will be with us. We need someone to care for her and make sure that she eats well as we will be visiting and socializing with friends in Europe.

Hilda smiled as she perused the picture of their daughter, Maxine, which they gave to her. A very beautiful, little girl, it seemed, as she said, "What a precious child." The Tate's eyes sparkled it seemed as they heard those words coming from Hilda.

Mrs. Tate immediately said, "Would you be willing to come to our home in Boston for the week-end and meet with our child. We would like to see how she would re-act to you being around for a couple of days. All of us, as a family, could talk and see how everyone gets along. Of course, we will pay your expenses eventhough you might not like the position after your interview in our home. We would like for you to depart with us on Friday a.m., as we plan to be back in Boston at that time. If you can do this, our chauffeur can pick you up at your apartment at 9: a.m. for the drive back to Boston. We hope that this meets with your approval because we think that you are the Nanny that we have been looking for.

Hilda could hardly contain herself. Nervously, she said, "I am sure that if this is what you and Mr. Tate would like for me to do, I will plan on these arrangements. Of course, we haven't talked about salary but I am sure that you will treat me in the right manner. Mrs. Tate retorted quickly, saying, "I am so sorry, but we have been paying all expenses when incurred by us, like trips, uniforms, that is if you want to wear uniforms, but not mandatory. The basic salary will be $500.00 a month and you live as a member of our family with your own room and bath. I have just recently had your bedroom and bath re-decorated and I am sure that it will meet with your approval.

Hilda smiling said, "I will be ready for your chauffeur to pick me up Friday a.m. You will find my address on the application given to you by the receptionist. Also, I want to thank you very much for the interview."

Mr. and Mrs. Tate shook her hand and out the door Hilda proceeded to the street to hurry home to give Lenora the good news. Hilda was hoping that this would be the position that she had been seeking but most of all she would be that much nearer to her daughter, Gloria.

On the way to the apartment, many things were going through Hilda's mind. She hoped that this was the right move for her. She had taken a taxi part of the way and then decided that she needed to have some exercise. Approaching the apartment, she saw Rogerio's taxi parked in front. Entering the foyer of the building, she could hear talking audible enough to realize that Lenora and Rogerio must be upset with each other. She knocked on the door before going in thinking that this might give them a chance to compose themselves.

As Lenora opened the door, both her and Rogerio had expressions of surprise and disgust. Lenora tried her best to act as if everything was ok but the tears in her eyes painted a different picture. Rogerio immediately dismissed himself and upon leaving said, "Lenora, I will call you later in the afternoon." Lenora was quiet as a mouse and stared at him as he left.

Hilda had proceeded to her room during all this and as the door closed on Rogerio, she came out and came over to Lenora and gave her a great big hug.

Hilda said, "I am not going to pry into your private life but when I arrived, I knew something had happened to upset you. I could tell by the expression on your beautiful face. If you want to discuss it, fine and if not, that is ok, too. I just want you to have a happy life,"

Lenora broke down and sobbed heavily. Yet, after a good cry, she still would not go into what had happened. Hilda said, "Well, if you don't want to talk to me, let me tell you what happened to me today. I made a commitment to further interview for this position in Boston. Their chauffeur will pick me up Friday 9 a.m. for a ride to their home in Boston for two or three days stay. Their daughter is five years of age and they want to see how she and I will get along. I am really looking forward to this position eventhough it might not be for only a few weeks covering their tour of Europe. It will give me a chance to travel without any expense. The couple will be paying for everything. Upon meeting them, I automatically liked them very much which I hope is a good omen." Hilda stopped talking and noticed Lenora's expression, as her eyes were filled with remorse.

Lenora seemed choked up as she said, "I don't know what to say. Of course, I am happy for you if this is your cup of tea. I know you will be good at what you do and most probably very happy. You have always seemed to be a person that would get along with most everyone. You were that kind of person in high school. It was very difficult for me to get along with my friends in high school but everyone loved you. Of course, you had a family that loved you dearly but my Mother and Daddy couldn't even get along with each other. I know now that means so much when growing up. I will hate to see you leave when you have only been here just a few days. But, you will write me from all those fancy places that you will be visiting."

Hilda gave her another hug and said, "I will let you hear how everything goes. If it is alright with you, I will pack all of my belongings, so that if I decide to accept the position, then I can have them picked up by their chauffeur at a later date. When they pick me up Friday, I am going to talk with them about this arrangement at that time. As mentioned earlier by them, they are in the big city several times a week."

By now, Lenora had composed herself. She said, "We'll have to celebrate tomorrow night and have dinner at The Tavern. I want to plan a very nice little dinner just for you and one of my friends is going to pick up the tab."

Hilda quickly said, "Lenora, you don't have to do all this just for me. I would be just as happy spending the last evening with just you and I talking."

"I know that would be nice but I want you have one big fling before you leave New York," quipped Lenora. Hilda didn't know what to say to Lenora as she seemed so adamant about her plan.

Hilda nodded her head to Lenora and then moved about the room saying, "I must get my clothes in order, especially those I am carrying with me Friday. My other things, I will pack in the large bag to be picked up, if I decide to accept the job after seeing that precious little girl. I do hope that everything will be in my favor so I can call Poppa that I have a position. He will be surprised that it will be in Boston and not New York City."

Since Friday was only day after tomorrow, Hilda felt that she should get a move on to be prepared. Moving around in the bedroom, Lenora had been so kind in letting her occupy since coming to New York, she felt that maybe she should leave a gift of money upon leaving on Friday. Really, in her heart she felt like this was going to be the position needed to get her started on the road to being closer to her baby girl. The more she thought of the position, she felt more confident that she would not be coming back to New York.

Lenora called her from the bedroom because she was going to make sure that everything was settled for an evening on the town. Hilda came into the living room saying, "Lenora, I must start getting my things organized for Friday and if you are still adamant about going out on the town, tonight will be alright. Because tomorrow night I would like to stay in and rest up for that trip Friday."

Lenora's eyes lit up, commenting, "Great, I will call Rogerio our plans and he can drop us off at the Tavern to start off the evening." Quickly, Hilda said, "Why don't you just include him in our plans for the evening. He might enjoy being with two women for the evening."

Hilda could tell by the expression on Lenora's face that she didn't want it that way, so she said, "Whatever you want to do is ok by me." Lenora snapped back, "Really, I want this to be a relaxing evening and who knows how many of my other friends I might see. Hilda retorted, "Ok, make your plans, just so we have a lovely outing." Lenora seemed happy, saying, "I have everything planned so just string along with me for the evening." Hilda smiled at Lenora saying, "Well, I am going to take a short siesta before getting ready for the evening."

Lying in her bed, Hilda wondering just what to expect from the evening ahead, she fell asleep. She awoke about 5 P.M., dazed from the good rest she had received. She sat on the edge of the bed wondering how she should dress for the evening.

A knock on Hilda's door and in walked Lenora all dressed as Hilda had never seen her before. Hilda thought to herself, I will not be able to compete with her this evening. Hilda said, "How beautiful you look tonight. That dress must have set you back a pretty penny. Lenora said, "Honey, I would never have been able to buy this dress. It was a gift certificate from one of my friends and I went down to a little shop on 5th Avenue and picked it out. Now, I want you to dress yourself up because tonight you will meet several of my friends who have been so generous since my arrival in the big city."

Hilda smiled at Lenora and said, "I will do my best but I want be able to outshine you tonight, because you look gorgeous."

Lenora left the room and Hilda dressed for the evening. About 6 PM, Hilda came out in the best she had brought to New York. Of course, it was the little black dress which was always the answer to every woman's dream. Matching jewelry and her hair put in a bouffant style on top of her head, which accentuated her long neck, made Lenora look second rate. Lenora could easily see that and as Hilda approached her in the living room, her expression on her overly made up face was obvious.

Lenora said, "You look great, Rogerio is on his way and should be here anytime. I don't want you to worry about anything this evening as everything has been taken care of. Rogerio will drop us off at the Tavern and we will be joined by several of my friends. Some of them, I am sure you will like and others you will not. Anyway I want you to have a great evening before you depart on your journey further up East.

Hilda just smiled and relaxed herself, waiting for Rogerio to show up. He arrived with several knocks on the door, which Lenora ignored. He walked in saying, "Ladies, I would love to join you but I have too many customers out there waiting for my services. But, I do hope you both have a lovely evening. I will be at your service if needed anytime tonight."

After departing for the Tavern, not a word was said by anyone. Arriving at the tavern, Hilda noticed that Lenora was saying something to Rogerio but she couldn't hear it as she had proceeded toward the entrance of the restaurant. When Lenora joined her on the way inside, Lenora said, "Sometimes I wonder why I don't just drop him completely but I wouldn't have any transportation when I needed it."

Lenora's expression seemed like she was waiting for a comment from Hilda but Hilda said nothing. Hilda didn't want to comment because Lenora had not confided in her their relationship. Hilda felt that she knew what was going on, the old expression, "Who is using who?"

Hilda followed Lenora as they proceeded further into the restaurant. Lenora followed the waiter into another room and as they entered, Hilda saw several people, completely strangers to her but not to Lenora, it seemed. There was much hugging and kissing going on between Lenora and these men and women. As Lenora introduced Hilda as her friend from home, all seemed very nice and a very touchy bunch.

Hilda noticed a wet bar on one side of the room and it seemed that they had been drinking for some time. Some of the men and women seemed very loose physically and mentally. Several asked Hilda if she was in the modeling business or trying to get into show business. They were surprised when she told them that she was becoming a "Nanny". They seemed very surprised and so did Lenora, because she didn't appreciate Hilda telling them. Lenora whispered to Hilda, "Why didn't you tell them you were trying out for a play on Broadway? Hilda remarked quickly, "Why should I lie? I don't know these friends of yours so why should I not say who I am? Hilda could tell Lenora was not happy with what she had said. Anyway, Hilda chatted with several people, limiting herself to one glass of wine.

It was about 8 PM before in waltzed the waiters with platters of food. As the waiters walked in they began to sing an old favorite, "So Long It Has Been Good To Know You," a song that had been kicked around Broadway for a number of years.

Lenora singing, quickly joined Hilda and several of the friends she had invited to Hilda's going away party. Much hugging and more touching, because it seemed that everyone had consumed enough drinks to be very relaxed. At least Hilda thought so because many of Lenora's friends were very friendly toward her, much more so than at the beginning of the evening. Hilda noticed that Lenora had several admirers vying for her attention. Sometimes she would say something to them not very audible to everyone but by the positive shake of their heads communication had been completed.

CHAPTER SIX

Lenora came over to Hilda and said, "I will be back shortly. I must go back to the apartment and change my dress. As you can see I have spilled something on it and need to get it off quickly or it will ruin the color.

Hilda said, "Do you want me to go with you. Are you calling Rogerio to come and take you there? Quickly Lenora said, "No, I have a friend that has consented to take me there. I shouldn't be long and this is your party, so carry on for me." In a way, Hilda was stunned but she gave her a positive shake of her head.

Hilda thought to herself, well, I must act properly and she made an effort to go around and say hello to everyone again. After awhile, she looked at her watch. It had been over an half hour since Lenora has excused herself. Hilda said to herself, hoping, "She will be back soon." An hour passed and still no Lenora. She felt that she couldn't leave the party. What would all of Lenora's friends think? At this stage, Hilda didn't really care about her friends. Many of them were really getting soused as we say down South.

As Hilda turned around to peruse the crowd, to see where all the cheering was coming from, in walked Lenora with three of her men friends that had been invited. Lenora had changed her dress and her facial expression was different than Hilda had ever seen. First, Hilda thought, she had consumed too many drinks because she seemed wobbly on her feet.

She stumbled over to Hilda saying, "Thanks, darling for carrying on for me while I was away. Turning around from Hilda, saying to the others, "I hope you all missed me but I was in good hands." The three guys who had chaperoned her back and forth laughed and smiled at everyone.

Lenora reaching for Hilda's hand, said to her, "Will you accompany me to the ladies' room? Hilda braced her as they left out of the room. On the way, Lenora said, "Hilda, do you have a purse?" Before she could answer, Lenora reached into her bosom and came out with a wad of bills, giving them to Hilda, saying, "Put these in your purse." Hilda was confused but did as Lenora requested saying, "You have some explaining to do when we get back to the apartment." Lenora commented, "Yes, I know I have lots to confess to you when we return, just do as I ask for now."

Hilda immediately said, "I am getting bushed and really need to go and get some rest. It is now 2 PM." Lenora holding to the edge of a table said, "You are not the only one, I will give Rogerio a call and we should be out of here in 30 minutes or so. Hilda took the arm of Lenora and they walked toward the foyer of the restaurant. Lenora found a telephone on a desk amid all the decorations and called Rogerio.

He must have not been far away because to Hilda it seemed he was there within five minutes. Lenora wasn't in a very good mood upon his arrival because it seemed that she did not have a very good time. She acted depressed and Hilda wondered why she had been gone for such a long time just to change her dress. She said not a word as she got into the taxi and neither did Rogerio. Hilda just observed all the body language that was going on. All she wanted to do this late was to get into bed for some sleep.

Rogerio got to the apartment faster than usual and not a word had been said by anyone. As Hilda got out of the taxi, she proceeded to the apartment and into her bedroom. Closing the door, she heard some loud talking coming from Lenora's bedroom and as she got into bed there were still audible noises coming from that direction. She was disturbed for awhile but finally fell asleep.

When Hilda woke up in the morning, she still felt tired. She knew that she had to get things together for next day when the Tates would pick her up for the ride to Boston. She was very happy about the whole situation especially after last night. She saw a different side of Lenora and was unhappy about finding out that really since her arrival in New York, what an unhappy person she must be. She was hoping that they would be able to talk awhile today and maybe she could help her in some way.

It was noon before Lenora showed her face and she was stunned as she approached the patio where Hilda was resting. Hilda had tried to get all of her belongings packed so if needed they could be picked up later. In Hilda's mind she really had decided to take the job in Boston if at all possible.

Lenora said, "I suppose you have been packing for tomorrow? I really don't want to think of you leaving but I know it's what you want to do. I should be proud for you but I hate to see you leave."

Hilda felt this was an opening for some deep conversation. She began by saying, "Lenora, you seem to be so depressed living here. Can you talk and tell me what is wrong? I know something hasn't been going just right for you, it seems. I am concerned because you and I are friends and if I can help, I want to." Hilda noticed that Lenora's facial expression changed several times as if trying to decide what to say.

Lenora completely fell apart as she fell into Hilda's arms. She was so full that the only thing Hilda heard were sobs beyond control. She clung to Hilda like a child. For a few minutes, nothing was said by either, just hugging profusely.

After awhile, both released each other and Lenora said, "I have much to confess to you because I want you to know what has happened to me since being in New York city. When I arrived in the city, after a few weeks and no job, I ran out of money. When I wrote home or called, my parents refused to help me. As you know, my parents don't have much extra money. Well, in the first month, I met several people who had money and they would wine and dine me. Some of these people, the men, after awhile would want something more than just my company. So I would wind up in bed with them and several are still giving me money. Rogerio has been paying the rent for sometime. You know that money had to come from somewhere, just like last night, when I asked you to put a wad of money in your purse. Well, that was the reason I was gone so long from the party. I am sorry I left you so long with a bunch of people that you didn't even know. I hope you will forgive me. Also, I have misrepresented my self as a working girl. I don't have a damn job and haven't had one since I arrived three years ago. Men friends and a few women have been keeping me up all this time. I know you hate me for this but I had to survive because I never did find a job that I liked."

Hilda looked at her, saying, "Lenora, what I really think you should do is take a vacation and spend sometime with your family back in Mississippi. After that, if you really want to come back to the big city, then you would be in a better position to make a decision. If you don't have the money to return home, I will give it to you. You really need a rest away from all this right now."

Lenora started crying and through muffled words, "You mean that you would give me money to return home for a visit?" Hilda quickly replied, "Yes, gladly." Lenora retorted, "Well, let me sleep on it tonight and will give you an answer tomorrow. There would be so much planning I would need to do before I left this burg."

Looking from the patio, Hilda could see the sun was setting behind the big buildings of the city and wondering what would tomorrow bring for her in Boston. She stood and said, "Lenora, I am going to get some rest and we'll talk again tomorrow before I leave.

Back in her room, she just couldn't believe what Lenora had confessed to her. All this time in New York she had accomplished nothing, just had a good time. Her good looks had faded some, but she was still a strikingly beautiful woman. But what concerned Hilda most was the hard expression she would show at times. When women lead this kind of a life, they usually get a no-care attitude and don't take care of themselves. As yet, this hadn't happened to Lenora. Maybe she would go home and not come back.

Hilda didn't open her bedroom door until about ten o'clock the next morning because she was getting everything in order just in case she didn't return. She felt her things would be picked up by the Tate Chauffeur as soon as she gave them a positive answer about accepting the nanny position. Many ways, Hilda felt this was her destiny at this stage of her life. It was time for her to move on toward getting closer to know her daughter, Gloria.

Lenora was sitting in the living room when Hilda came out with her small bag that she was going to take with her to Boston. She said, "Lenora, I meant what I said last evening about giving you a gift of money for you to visit your folks back in Mississippi."

Lenora quickly said, "I really don't feel that I can go back just at this time but I appreciate the gesture. Can I take a rain check on that offer?

Hilda looked surprised and said, "You know you can, just let me know when. Are you sure you want to go back home for a visit? I still think it would be a good idea. I really think that it is time for you to change your life style. You may not like for me to talk to you this way but I care, after all we have been friends for quite a few years."

Lenora started crying and Hilda could hardly understand her muttered voice saying, "I know what I have been doing is not good for me but I wonder just how I would fare back home. I probably would get bored and aggravate my parents. I will keep in touch with you when you get settled or whatever in Boston."

All of a sudden both women got quiet because several knocks could be heard on the front door. Lenora, wiped her eyes, and opened the door, there stood a tall man dressed in a uniform. He said, "Do you have a Miss Webber here? I have been instructed by Mr. and Mrs. Tate to pick her up for their drive to Boston."

Lenora looked around toward Hilda and she said, "I am Miss Webber and I'm ready. Would you please get my luggage over there by the door. The man said, "I am Regis, the Tate's chauffeur, at your service." Picking up the bag, he said, "I will be standing by the limo when you come out."

Hilda and Lenora embraced, nothing said but they stared at each other as Hilda left the apartment. Walking toward the three door limo, Regis was standing by the door to open it. As she approached, in military fashion he opened the door. Seating herself, her mind began to wonder, these folks must be wealthy. She felt like a celebrity being catered to in this fashion.

As the limo pulled off, Regis said, "I am going to pick up Mr. and Mrs. Tate at the hotel and then we will be on our way to

Boston. Mrs. Tate informed me that you are going to be their daughter's new Nanny. Their child is a beautiful little girl almost 6 or 7 years of age with cold black hair. The only thing is that they can't control her very well and I do hope that you will be able to do something about that. The child has a very independent attitude, very smart, already plays the piano very well but doesn't get along well with her peers. I hope you don't mind me telling you all this because I felt that you should know what you have on your hands. I would appreciate it, if you would not mention to the Tates what I have told you."

"Regis, may I call you Regis?", came out of Hilda's mouth before she could control herself. "I will not mention a word of our discussion and I want you to feel that I am your friend. Anytime that you wish to discuss anything, please feel free to do so. We, if I accept the position, both of us will be their employees, so let's be friends. I am here on a trial basis, I am sure, to see how I get along with the child for a few days. The child's name is Maxine, is that correct? He quickly replied, "Yes and such a pretty name for a little girl."

To Hilda, the man seemed intelligent, educated and probably from another country. His personality was different from the young southern men she had encountered. Actually, he was more handsome than her first love, Anthony Leo.

As she rode along the streets to the hotel to where the Tates were waiting for them, her mind drifted back to the time she first laid eyes on Anthony and her first kiss from him was all she needed to fall in love. She wondered would she ever find a man that she could marry and have a family.

Hilda came back to reality as the limo pulled up to the entrance of the New Yorker Hotel. Regis said, "Just sit for a spell, I will be back as soon as I get the Tates and their luggage."

Almost immediately, Hilda saw the Tates coming toward the limo and Regis opened the third side door and they seated themselves, leaving Hilda sitting in the middle by herself. The Tates seemed to be in a good mood, smiling, with Mrs. Tate saying, "We are so glad that you have decided to come be with us for a few days. I know Maxine will be expecting us this evening and we have informed the servants to plan a nice meal for all of us. We have missed Maxine so much the last three days. A friend has been caring for her while we were away. But, Maxine needs a full time Nanny and you will agree once you are around her for awhile. We hope that you and her get along from the beginning.

Hilda swiveled her seat around saying, "I am sure she is a sweet, little girl, almost all children are. I want to observe her and see what makes her tick then I can tell you my opinion. As you know because I am sure you checked my credentials before I got this far, that I have a teacher's certification. Let's wait and see what happens in the next few days. Then, I can be more truthful about the matter of you employing me for your daughter.

Regis turned around for a moment and asked if anyone needed a break. He said that we should be home in about an hour. No one wanted to stop, so he kept driving toward Boston.

The Tates talked a lot about their upcoming travels to Europe. They were excited about going and everything they mentioned, Hilda noticed that they included her in the scenario. In Hilda's mind, it was not set in concrete that she was going to accept this position. Of course, everything mentioned sounded great and getting to travel was just a bonus.

Actually, Hilda had high hopes for this position but she didn't want to seem over anxious. The Tates informed her that they lived part of the year in Boston and part of the year in their townhouse in Hartford, Connecticut. Maybe she might be able to make some good contacts while working for the Tates even if it was for only a short period of time. This might be a way for her to get to know something about the Langleys in Hartford who had adopted her daughter. Of course, Hilda was too busy otherwise to think of this situation, so to herself she thought, I will worry about that tomorrow.

Everyone seemed to be weary from talking and as Hilda peered out the limo window, she could see homes, expensive homes on spacious grounds. It wasn't long before the limo pulled off the street into a very well manicured, spacious yard with a driveway which took at least fifteen minutes to get into the back garage of this gorgeous townhouse. As Regis parked, Hilda could see three cars in the huge carport. Hilda thought, these people have money and plenty of it.

The Tates waited for Regis to open the limo doors so all could disembark. Hilda was lead by Mrs. Tate's hand into a small elevator in the garage and up they went to the first floor of the townhouse. When the elevator stopped and door opened, Hilda could see a large oil painting hanging on the foyer wall. She understood what Regis meant when he said that she was a beautiful child. Hilda had a lump in her throat as she thought of her daughter, Gloria, wondering if she would be that beautiful.

A housemaid approached Mrs. Tate and said, "As soon as everyone can get settled, dinner will be served. Just let me know when." Mrs. Tate nodded her head and told everyone that as soon as they were ready to come to the dining room. Mrs. Tate said to Hilda, "Maxine will join us for dinner and then you will get to meet her. Also, your bag has been carried to your room and your maid will show you where it is located. In a few minutes everyone will go to the dining room."

Hilda followed the maid up a staircase, down the hall a bit, into a huge room which was to be her bedroom, sitting area and private bath. The bathroom was as big as her bedroom back in D'Lo. She was impressed, perusing the layout, little private sitting room, and a bedroom within the huge room. She got her bag and put it in the bedroom, saying to herself, I will attend to that later because I am hungry. Checking her face and freshening her hands, she proceeded back the same way she came up. When she got to the bottom of the staircase, the Tates were waiting for her and they all went into the dining area.

As Hilda walked into the dining room, she heard Maxine laughing. She thought, what a wonderful laugh. Hilda kneeled down by the child's chair, saying, "Hello, I am Miss Hilda and I bet you are Maxine." The child just stared at Hilda as if to be under Hilda's spell and in a moment, smiling, said, "Miss Hilda, I am so glad that you are visiting with us." Hilda said, "I hope you and I will have lots of fun in the next few days."

The Tates were beside themselves as to Maxine's action which showed on their facial expressions. As everyone seated themselves, not a thing was discussed relative to what had happened because Hilda knew it would be discussed later. Maxine acted as if she was starved for attention and Hilda agreed.

The Tates didn't talk very much during dinner. Hilda followed suit because they acted like that was not the thing to do and as she glanced a smile every now and then at Maxine, she would drop her head.

CHAPTER SEVEN

After dinner Mr. and Mrs. Tate asked Hilda to follow them into the living room. As Hilda followed along, Maxine came up and took her hand. As everyone seated themselves, Maxine was still holding on to Hilda's hand.

Mrs. Tate said, "Maxine, come and sit by Mother and let Miss Hilda rest for a spell. She has had a long ride today." Maxine reluctantly moved over and sat between her Mom and Dad but Hilda could easily tell the child was not happy doing so.

Hilda said, "It's ok, the child is not annoying me. She is only trying to make me feel welcome in a childish way. This is very good for the relationship between us because if I accept the position, there will be times when she will depend upon me to guide her in her decision making. This is "Child Psychology 404" which I studied in college."

The Tates looked at each other with a smile of approval. Mrs. Tate said, "Maxine's bedroom is right across the hall from yours. Mr. Tate and I hope that you will be able to give us an answer as soon as possible. Much work is yet to be done by us before we finalize the trip which has been reserved for several months. As we discussed, you and Maxine will be sharing the same suite as you will be in charge of her for the entire excursion. We already feel that you are the right person for this trip so now it is left up to you to give us an answer."

Hilda immediately said, "I will let you know tomorrow morning. Just let me sleep on it tonight and then I can have a fresh outlook on this situation. I want to do what is best for you and Mr. Tate but more importantly for the child."

Both Mr. and Mrs. Tate came over to Hilda and bade them good night. Mrs. Tate said, "Hilda, I feel that you will take charge and make our home, your home. So adieu for now until tomorrow.

Hilda came over and took Maxine by the hand and they were off to bed, saying good night to everyone. Maxine went along with Hilda as if she had done this before. She seemed pleased to be happy in her situation.

Upon arriving upstairs, Hilda took Maxine into her bedroom suite and they chatted awhile. Maxine said, "I love talking with you before I go to bed. I have been wishing that I had someone that I could be close to and play with. Are you going to stay awhile and take care of me. Mommy said, "You could if you wanted to and I hope you do," as she moved closer to Hilda and gave her a hug.

Hilda said to herself, "This child is starved for attention and if I stay, I will see that she gets her share." Maxine moved around in the room showing things to Hilda. Hilda said, "Don't you think we should be going to bed?" Maxine said, "Yes, come on over to my room and then you can tuck me in. Sometimes Mommy and Daddy tuck me in but not very often. The last lady that took care of me was hateful but I never mentioned it to Mommy and Daddy because they were not here very much. It seems they were always gone."

Maxine took Hilda's hand and motioned for her to come with her. Hilda had not perused Maxine's room very well when Mrs. Tate showed it to her upon arrival. When Maxine opened the door to her room, it would be very difficult to believe that a child could not be happy with such beautiful surroundings. This child had everything but a true sense that she was loved. She was starved for attention.

Acting much more mature than her age. Maxine showed Hilda where her clothes were located, including her night gown. She even proceeded to get herself ready for bed as she went to a chest and came back with a gown.

Hilda said, "Come over here and sit down by me and I will help you with your nightie." Maxine's face lit up as she giggled handing the gown to Hilda. Hilda helped her and combed her hair, gave her a big hug saying, "Up we go now to bed." Maxine ran to her bed and as Hilda approached she noticed tears in Maxine's eyes. Hilda bent over and kissed her on the cheek saying, "Maxine, I will be right behind that door, if you need me. I love you child. I believe you want me to stay around for awhile and if you do I will think about it until tomorrow." Maxine said, "Oh, please stay, Miss Hilda. I know that I will sleep like a fairy tonight, so goodnight." Hilda walking toward the door to her bedroom, said, "Goodnight, see you tomorrow."

Hilda, upon arriving in her bedroom, sat down to take inventory of the day's events. So much was going through her mind. One confusing thing was when she first arrived at the Tates' home there was a black couple at the home. She was not introduced to them and only saw them at a distance as they were leaving. The couple seemed very well dressed and she noticed they left in a very upscale sports car. Hilda could come to only one conclusion, that they were friends of the Tates. She thought to herself, this is above the Mason-Dixon Line, not in D'Lo and white and blacks do socialize with each other. Since she had come to New York, many of the people she had met had mixed marriages. This didn't bother Hilda because she knew that her daughter had been adopted by a black couple. Again, she said to herself, "As God is my witness, I will see my baby girl one of these days."

The next morning, Mrs. Tate knocked on Hilda's door. Hilda said, "Come on in and let's go over the schedule for the day so I will have an idea as to what kind of a day to plan for Maxine. I am a firm believer that there should be some kind of an academic schedule for the morning time. She is old enough to be taught some form of reading, writing and being able to count. Then, after lunch, she should have a quiet time, maybe a short nap and then before bed time, play some games. This plan has seemed to work for children her age. What do you think of the plan that I have laid out? Please feel free to discuss whatever but I have to have control of whatever I do for the sake of the child."

Mrs. Tate smiled at Hilda, saying, "Please let's sit for a moment. Miss Webber, or may I call you Hilda?" Quickly Hilda said, "Don't you think it would be better if you call me, Miss Hilda or Miss Webber, because of Maxine. This would make an impression of good rapport between us." Mrs. Tate shaking her head in approval, said, "Of course, it would be the right thing to do. Miss Webber, I am convinced that you would be good for my child and do you have any idea that you could take the position. I will see that you have complete control over the plan that you have proposed. The chauffeur will return to the apartment in New York tomorrow and retrieve your luggage as we planned if you just say the word, Yes."

Hilda seemed to be stunned for a moment. She looked straight into Mrs. Tate's eyes, saying, "Do you think that I could return with your chauffeur to get my luggage and be able to say goodby to my friend properly. She is from my home town back in Mississippi and was very kind to me while visiting her. Maybe Maxine could ride with me on the trip."

Seemingly overjoyed, Mrs. Tate said, "Of course, you can do that and take Maxine with you. I suppose this means yes. Oh, I am so relieved that you are going to look out for Maxine. I will tell Regis to prepare for an early morning trip. Also, as of now Regis is at your disposal for you to take Maxine whenever you desire for drives through the countryside. Of course, this time next week we will be on the high seas toward Europe. I know you will enjoy this month long tour and I know that I will since I will have you looking after Maxine."

Hilda got up and told Mrs. Tate that she would go check on Maxine. She found Maxine still in bed and as she approached her bed she held out her arms for Hilda to hug her. Hilda felt at that moment that she had made the right decision about accepting the position because of Maxine. She was so eager for love and attention in her life. Thoughts of her child, Gloria, clouded her mind.

Hilda didn't see Mrs. Tate for the remainder of the day as she was planning for the trip abroad. But, Regis was in the front foyer as she came down with Maxine for a mid-morning snack. When he saw Hilda, he said, "Ms. Webber, I have been advised by the Tates that I am to drive you into the big city tomorrow. You let me know when we are to leave. All you have to do is contact me on the house communication system and I will be ready whenever you wish. I have been informed that I am to be your body guard while employed here, so I am to be at your beck and call.

Hilda said, "Regis, thanks for your advice and understanding. The Tates are now busy getting prepared for their trip abroad since I have consented to be Maxine's nanny. On our trip to New York tomorrow we will have time to talk. I am sure you will be able to give me answers to questions that I need to know."

The thoughts concerning Regis came flooding into Hilda's mind. He was so kind and gentle, she wanted to know more about him. To herself, she said, "Until tomorrow, I have lots to do this afternoon."

Maxine got her attention by saying, "I want to go up to my play room and find a toy that I would like to take on our trip. Hilda caught her small hand and up they went to wherever Maxine was carrying her. As they neared a door, Maxine said, "Guess where we are?" Hilda's rebuttal was, "Let me guess. Don't tell me. I bet there are lots of toys behind that door." Maxine screamed with laughter saying, "You must have peeked already because your are so right."

Opening the door, Hilda was amazed at so many different toys and gadgets. She sat down on the floor and just watched Maxine take over the whole room. Again, she thought of her child, Gloria, wondering if she was having fun like Maxine. Maxine went to one corner of the room and brought back a little clown doll which she handed to Hilda. Hilda said, "Is this your favorite? Maxine looking down at the floor. looked up at Hilda with tears in her eyes, saying, "He was lonely, like me, but we want be anymore since your are going to stay with us. His name is Freddy and I want to take him with me on the trip if they will let me. Miss Webber, you ask them for me."

Hilda replied, "Maxine, I don't see any reason why they will not let you take Freddy. But you know you will have to look after him for the entire trip. If he is left behind somewhere he will be lonely."

Trying to understand why Maxine was lonely, confused Hilda. A child with loving parents or at least they seem that way and having all the material things needed is difficult to understand why she would be lonely. There must be something lacking that she must find out, maybe tomorrow on the trip, Regis will enlighten her about the Tates. Of course, she will have to know more about Regis before questioning him. He might not understand and talk to the Tates about her talking with him about their private business. Of course, she was still wondering why and how Regis obtained his employment with the Tates.

The next morning was a hustle and bustle, it seemed to Hilda. She had been told at breakfast by Mrs. Tate that Regis would be ready to leave for New York by 9: AM which left her about an hour to get everything in order including Maxine. Mrs. Tate didn't show any interest other than making sure that Hilda had her on the agenda for the day. Hilda knew it would be an all day trip but why was it so important that Maxine go with her. Maxine was running from her room to Hilda's every few minutes making sure that she was included in everything. Hilda could see already that the child would rather be with her than her Mother. Maxine would be very disappointed if she had been told that the trip was off.

Regis was downstairs waiting when Hilda and Maxine arrived. He said, "Do you have anything that you want me to put in the limo? Also, here is an envelope Mrs. Tate said for me to give to you. The Tates left earlier to confirm something about the trip next week. Hilda took the envelope, saying, "I don't think we will need anything that I know of for our drive into the city, just to retrieve my luggage."

Regis walked outside with Hilda and Maxine following behind. He immediately opened the limo door for Hilda and Maxine. Hilda got situated inside the limo with Maxine. As they were departing the Tate compound, she looked back wondering what experiences were in store for her in this situation. Out upon the main highway driving toward the big city, Maxine became less talkative and fell asleep. Every now and then Hilda noticed that Regis would glance back at her in the mirror. For the first time she felt that maybe he was trying to flirt with her. She didn't want her curiosity to get the upper hand until she could openly talk with him. She just relaxed and watched Maxine enjoy her sleep.

At a long red light, Regis turned around sharply saying, "Would you like to move up here in the front seat so we can talk without awakening Maxine?

For a moment Hilda was stunned but composing herself she said, "Do you think that stopping the car would awaken her? Regis said, "No, I don't think so, maybe arouse her for a moment." Hilda said, "Ok, that would be nice to be able to engage in a little conversation." "You maybe bored with my conversation," he said. I doubt that very much," she said.

Immediately he pulled over in front of a nearby service station. Jumping out quickly, he opened the door and Hilda got in the front seat. Maxine didn't seem to notice what was happening. Regis pulled the big limo back into the highway traffic without saying a word.

Hilda couldn't keep the silence, so she began by saying, "Regis, tell me all about yourself, what you do when not working etc.? When you get through, I will tell you about this Mississippi girl."

Regis seemed ill at ease at first but after a few sentences he started laughing as he talked. He said, "I am from a small town in Belgium and came to America right after graduating from college which was five years ago. The Tates hired me through an employment agency and have spent the last two years in their employment. Before that I entered college but run out of money and had to go to work. As you probably can tell, I will soon be 30 years of age. I studied acting but it is more difficult to break into the theatre here than in Europe. My family wanted me to return home but salaries are less in Belgium than in America. Anyway, I like living in America and one day I will get my chance to show those producers in the big city that I have talent. I am trying to save up enough money to survive for one year while I try a few auditions there. Maybe after another year, I will be able to venture out."

Hilda's mind was running rampant because she had a different idea relative to Regis. She knew he was handsome, talked very precisely and moved like an athlete but never did she think he was interested in being an actor.

Looking at Hilda, Regis said, "It's you turn to tell me about that good looking girl from Mississippi."

Hilda giggled saying, "I don't have to tell you I am from the southern part of the United States. You have heard my southern accent already." Raising his hand as if to say stop, he said, "What is wrong with your accent? I like the way you say things. They seem so easy and fluid. When in acting school, we had to imitate you and it was very difficult but with you it seems so natural. Most people like to hear southerners talk."

Hilda said, "I am one year younger than you if you are really 30. I graduated from a Teachers college and that is why I took this position with the Tates. They wanted someone to go with them on their trip next week to take care of Maxine. I have only committed myself to them for the time of the trip. Then, after that I have no idea what will be my destiny. Some where another nanny position will come along. I can always go back to my home in Mississippi and my Poppa will take care of me. I have the most wonderful man as a father, I call him "Poppa." That is just another southern colloquialism."

Regis broke into her conversation, saying, "Maybe I shouldn't say this, but for the child's sake I am glad that you are here for Maxine. Anyone can tell she is a lonely child because her parents hardly ever spend a lot of time with her. They are always on the go keeping up with society functions. As you can see the Tates are very wealthy and seem to have an over abundance of outside activity. I am telling you all of these things and maybe I shouldn't because the Tates might not approve of me talking to you about their family."

"Since you have relaxed me a bit, Regis, tell me more about the Tates," commented Hilda. "Don't worry about me talking with them about our conversation, I, too, am an employee," said Hilda.

Regis was quiet for a few moments and then he said, "Well, since you are a person of the south, firstly, you will see mixed couples visiting the Tates as some of their best friends are African Americans. I noticed this upon my first day of employment. Of course, this doesn't bother me in any way since I am from Europe. I believe you are educated enough that it will not bother you either. Another thing, they entertain a lot and sometimes way into the wee hours of the morning. That is one reason why you don't see them until after mid-day. I hope you don't feel offended by me telling you all this information but I felt that you needed to know. By the way, did you open your envelope that I gave you when we started on the drive?"

Hilda jittery seeing the envelope, reaching to the back seat and opening it, she pulled out two one hundred dollars bills with a note, saying, "This is for you and Maxine to spend on the trip today." Quickly Hilda said, "This will cover our expenses for the day. You know the places to eat so I will leave that in your hands."

Regis immediately said, "I was thinking there was money in that envelope because they do the same for me when I take them on a visit to their friends or when they go out for an evening. You see I am on duty 24 hours a day, seven days a week. So now you know when you can get me as my apartment is in the basement. A phone is in your room if you ever need me, dial 44. I am at your service, madam." Hilda noticed with awe the smile he gave her when giving her instructions how to contact him.

So far, the drive into the big city was very pleasant. Maxine had slept most of the way and was now fully awake as they pulled up at Hilda's friend, Lenora's apartment. Before getting out, Hilda told Regis that she enjoyed the conversation and to think of some nice place for all of them to eat before leaving the big city.

When Hilda knocked on Lenora's door, she came bounding out of the apartment, throwing her arms around Hilda, almost knocking her down. Hilda immediately thought she had been drinking.

Lenora said, "Girl, have I missed you. You must stay here in the big city with me." Hilda came back quickly saying, "Lenora, at this time I have a good position and the child that I have in my care is with me in the limo. Come out and see a beautiful little girl."

They both walked outside where Regis was standing by the limo with Maxine. Lenora stood in awe when she saw Regis. Hilda asked Maxine to tell Lenora, "Hello." Maxine caught Hilda's hand and said, "Hello." Regis didn't budge until Hilda asked him to get her luggage which was just inside the door of the apartment. He moved with military agility with no questions asked.

As Regis left to get the luggage, Lenora said, "Do you see this man every day? Hilda said, "Yes, he is my employer's chauffeur."

Lenora retorted, "It would be a problem if I looked upon such a gorgeous man every day and not be able to touch him."

With the luggage in the limo, Hilda and Lenora were saying their goodbyes, Hilda said, "I will call you before I leave next week on the trip to Europe. Yes, we must keep in touch. As you know, I do not know how long I will be in this position."

Hilda and Maxine got into the limo and Regis closed the door. As the limo left the curb, Lenora was still waving good-by.

Riding along, Hilda said, "Regis, I apologize for my friend because I think she had a drink or two before we arrived. Also, find us a nice place to eat because it is past lunch time. Maxine has already told me that she was hungry." He turned around and smiled giving a positive nod.

Outside the city limits, the limo came to a stop in front of a seafood restaurant. Regis said, "I have stopped here with the Tates and the food was very good but expensive. I believe Maxine will enjoy the decorations of fish inside."

Regis jumped out with precision as usual opening the limo door. Hilda got out with Maxine holding her hand, commenting, "It sure looks like a nice place and I believe that I am hungry after glancing at my watch. It is after one o'clock and I know this poor child is starved. Regis, I bet you could eat a big seafood platter."

Regis smiled, saying, "Usually, I never turn down good seafood which they have in this part of the world. My favorite is lobster thermidor or stuffed crabs."

Hilda said, "I haven't eaten much lobster but back home we always have plenty of cat fish, crab cakes or fried shrimp. Nothing better, except southern fried chicken." Maxine took it all in as they were talking, laughing and smiling all the time.

After eating, they were on their way again to Boston and not long after settling down, Maxine fell asleep. Noticing that Maxine was now asleep, Regis looked back and said, "Don't you want to come up front so we can talk? I may have a few more things to discuss or if you have questions, just ask. I am at your service, madam."

Hilda smilingly said, "Whenever you can stop, I will come up for a visit because I prefer not to doze all the way to Boston." Regis didn't take long to stop the limo. As usual, he jumped out and opened the door for her to enter the limo.

Hilda, getting relaxed since moving into the front seat with Regis, was more interested in what he might have to say. But before she could open her mouth, Regis said, "Have you been informed that there will be a huge party of the Tates' friends before leaving on the trip next week? Friends from here in Boston, Hartford, Connecticut and Old Orchard Beach, Maine will converge on the compound arriving early and staying late. I believe that it will be on Thursday before you all sail on the Queen Mary on Saturday at 4: PM. The Tates will leave no stone unturned for their friends, big band music, dancing, and much food and drink. You will enjoy the atmosphere, I hope."

Hilda commented quickly, "Have you attended one of these soirees or are we invited?"

Regis laughed, saying, "Really, they act like they wanted us to be present but, why, I don't know the answer. The Tates have only mentioned it to me casually. I am sure they will discuss this further with you when we return."

Regis looked at Hilda, smiling and then commented, "You being an educated person, though you are from the South, I am sure you will not be offended by the people who show up. There will be mixed couples, both black and white but very academic. Some of them I have talked with and they seem to be very nice. I am sure most of them have money or their life style is a flake."

Hilda's mind was running full speed ahead, wondering what would be the agenda the next few days, she said, "Regis, you and I will have to compare notes so that we will be able to keep each other informed. I appreciate your candor in helping me getting situated in my position. Anything we say will be just between us."

CHAPTER EIGHT

Regis nodded his head and said, "I am sure they will have a meeting with you and I when we arrive late this afternoon. By the way, I must say I have enjoyed the trip today and I hope there will be more when you return from the trip abroad."

Quickly Hilda said, "Honestly, I don't know how long I will be here because from what I understand, they only mentioned my employment for the length of trip. Their main idea was to have someone to take care of Maxine on their ocean voyage. But, I will do what I have to do to make it successful for them because they are paying me very well for my services."

Hilda looked straight into Regis' eyes and noted a sad expression seemed to have covered his usual smiling face. She wondered just what was going through his mind. Any way she felt at this time that she didn't have time for romance if that should be the case with him.

Regis broke the spell by saying, "We should be at the compound within thirty minutes. We'll see what the Tates have on the agenda for the rest of the afternoon. I know they mentioned earlier that they wanted to have a meeting with us and maybe it will be later today."

Hilda said, "Whatever they decide will be fine with me so I can plan according to Maxine. Mrs. Tate will have everything planned because she is very excited about this trip. Of course, I know it will be a nice vacation in some ways eventhough I will be working looking after Maxine." Trying to be nice, she quickly commented to Regis, "I wish you were going to be along to make the trip more interesting."

Regis smiled from ear to ear commenting very slowly, "Do you really feel that way? If so, we can resume where we left off, upon your return."

"I said it didn't I", Hilda saying laughingly. "This will give you something to occupy your mind while I am gone," retorted Hilda. Looking straight ahead she could see the Tate compound around the corner.

Regis pulled into the Tate compound and parked the limo. He got out quickly to open the door for Hilda and Maxine to disembark. Going to the limo trunk, he retrieved Hilda's luggage and left wth them going to her living quarters. Hilda and Maxine were met by Mrs. Tate almost immediately as they walked toward the house from the limo garage.

Mrs. Tate hugged Maxine saying, "Glad you both had a good trip. Looking at Hilda she said, "We will have a meeting with you and Regis at 7: PM for final plans on our trip. Dinner will be served at six and then our meeting in the large foyer. Glad you and Maxine had a safe trip."

Hilda thanked Mrs. Tate for the trip into the big city to retrieve her belongings. With Maxine in tow, she left for her room. She wanted to get a hot bath and change clothes for dinner. Maxine needed to take a short nap and then play while she was at the meeting.

After dinner, everyone adjourned to the large front foyer for the meeting with the Tate's. Hilda noticed several people that she had not seen before but Regis whispered to her that everyone here were employees.

Mr. and Mrs. Tate presided over the meeting. Mrs. Tate told everyone about the "going away party" that was to be held at the compound on Friday night before boarding the ship Sunday afternoon around 4: p.m. That meant that their guests would be staying around for two whole days. Some guests would be staying at the compound and some at local hotels. She laid out instructions so that everyone would know what responsibilities that would be needed. Mr. Tate told everyone that they would be expected to be on duty as usual each day until their return. Mr. Regis will be in charge while we are gone. Then, he said, "I will excuse everyone now so we can have a meeting with Miss Hilda and Regis."

After all had departed except Hilda and Regis, Mr. and Mrs. Tate asked one of the house waiters to serve everyone a glass of wine. You could tell Mrs. Tate was all aglow over the trip. She was very cordial and laughing at everything it seemed. She handed Hilda and Regis a sheet of paper saying, "These are our guests for the week-end party. Many of them have been our friends for many years and usually everyone of them show up. We want everyone of them to have a great time, plenty of eating, drinking and big band music. As you can see the foyer has become a band podium and plenty of space for dancing. Most of these people love to dance. If anyone has questions, please let us know and thanks for your cooperation."

Hilda, sitting there beside Regis, perused the guest list. Gazing down the list, she wondered about all these names and then all of a sudden the name jumped out at her, Mr. and Mrs. Jason Langley. She really had a fainty feeling as she read it over and over. In her mind, she wondered if this could possibly be the couple that had adopted her baby six years ago in Natchez, Mississippi. She heard Mrs. Tate saying, "Miss Hilda, I have already got Maxine's clothes packed. I let one of the maids pack her clothes while you were gone to the big city."

Hilda tried to get up but felt unsteady for a moment. She said, "Mrs. Tate, I know we are going to have a wonderful vacation because of your good planning. I am really looking forward to this trip almost as much as you are."

Mrs. Tate was all smiles, saying, "You are so kind, I just knew you were the person for Maxine to have on this trip."

Hilda said adieu to Regis and was off to her room to meditate for awhile. While sitting in her room as Maxine was already in bed, she thought to herself, "Could this be the same couple that was on her baby's adoption papers? If so, maybe by some hook or crook, one day she might be able to see her baby without anyone knowing that she is the mother. The couple has never seen her or know who she is because that was never put on the birth certificate. Her father had made sure that information was not recorded, only her father's name was put on the birth certificate. Unwed mothers in Mississippi were frowned upon and by mistake these things were left off birth certificates and adoption papers."

Any way, she felt sure that no children would be brought to this party with their parents for two days. Meeting the Langleys was uppermost in Hilda's mind at this moment and maybe she would by this time tomorrow evening.

Hilda hung out with Maxine most of the morning until her maid arrived. Thinking about the party beginning late in the afternoon, she said, "I want to bring out one of my slinky party dresses and have a good time tonight."

About 5: p.m. people began to show up and by 6: p.m. the foyer looked like a night club. The band had arrived earlier and were now playing that big band sound. Many tables had been moved in with table cloths and small lights on each. To Hilda it looked very festive and she let Mrs. Tate know it and she was very pleased.

Some of the guests were milling around, dancing and talking. As Mrs. Tate was introducing some of the couples to Hilda, in walked a very handsome light-skinned black couple which was introduced as Mr. and Mrs. Jason Langley. Hilda almost blacked out as she said, "Hello!" I am nanny to Mrs. Tate's daughter, Maxine." Mrs. Langley said, "Yes, Mrs. Tate has told me about you and how fortunate she was to secure your services especially for her trip. We have a beautiful daughter, also, who will soon be seven years of age. Our daughter is very special, smart, already plays the piano and dances like a ballerina. We are so fortunate to have her."

Hilda was in a dither, so she excused herself, saying, "Enjoyed meeting you and will see you later, I am sure." Hilda was still dizzy when she got inside of her room. She sat down thinking about her daughter, smart, plays the piano and can dance. Thinking in her mind, "I have missed all this with my baby." Tears overflowed her eyes as she threw herself on the bed. Lying there, she knew she had to get up and make her appearance at the party.

Downstairs she saw Regis and he motioned for her to join him at a small table over in a corner not too far from the band stand. He said, "Don't you just love this music. I could sit here all night if they would play that long. Do you want to dance?

Hilda got up without saying a word, Regis holding out his arms, she fell right into them. She was glad she had learned how to foxtrot while at Mississippi College. Most girls going there would not let anyone know that they really participated in any kind of dancing. Regis was good and Hilda was glad. Regis could dance slow or fast and that was right down Hilda's alley. Hilda and Regis caused quite a stir on the dance floor because some of the couples sat down to watch when they were on the dance floor.

After awhile, Mrs. Tate came forward and announced that dinner would be served in the adjoining room. Everyone marched in pairs into the very elaborate dining area led by the Tates. Regis and Hilda brought up the rear and sat at a table alone which suited them.

Regis said to Hilda, "We are just where we can watch everyone and yet be a part of what is happening." Hilda agreed with him, saying, "Many of my narrow minded friends would find grounds for criticism if they could observe all the whites and blacks socializing together at this party. Of course, as you know I am from the South but my family has always had blacks within our home. To this day, I have a black woman taking care of my Dad, or Poppa to me. She has been living within our household for years."

Regis told Hilda that the Tates went overboard in planning this party. He commented that this was the best one since his employment with them. He said that many of their friends were blacks but in Europe they called them negroes. Further, he commented that he never thought of any distinction relative to race until he came to America. Look at the people invited by the Tates, they all seem to be having a great time. Hilda did observe and she commented that several of them seem to be connected to the black race.

After eating, Mrs. Tate came by and greeted both Regis and Hilda. She wanted to know if they were enjoying themselves. Hilda told her that she had checked on Maxine with her nurse and she was already in bed. Mrs. Tate told them that tomorrow night, there would be entertainers with the band for the evening.

As she was preparing to leave them, she said, "Somebody has learned to do ballroom dancing well. You all seemed to be enjoying the music. She also commented to Hilda, "Mrs. Jason asked me if you would be in my employ upon returning from the trip. Hilda quickly said, "Why would she be asking such a question? Mrs. Tate said, "I think that she might have thought that you would be here just for the trip with Maxine. I had previously told her that I had employed a nanny for Maxine for the trip. There was no more discussion between us relative to the situation."

It was getting late, so Hilda told Regis that she would see him tomorrow sometime. She would be, up in her room, getting her bags organized and packed for the trip. The Tates were busy with their guests and having after dinner drinks so Hilda left for her room.

In her room, she started to wonder about Gloria. She still felt in her heart that she would be able to see her sometime soon, maybe sooner than expected. Getting in bed after a good, hot shower, she fell asleep. Drifting off in slumber, she could see her baby girl.

Next day was filled with people eating, talking and planning little side trips to see art exhibits, and taking tours to Province Town. Regis was a busy man with the limo and seeing Hilda, he asked if she would like to go with him on one of the tours. Hilda reneged because she had so much to do in her room. She told him that she would check with him later in the day.

Hilda, up in her room, tried to get clothes arranged for packing. She did a lot of thinking about her baby and wondered why Mrs. Jason had talked to Mrs. Tate about her employment. Was she looking for a nanny for her child? Would she hire a white lady since she was black to take care of her daughter? All these things were circling around in Hilda's mind. Of course, she had no one to discuss them with so it was very difficult for her. So as usual, she said to herself, "I will worry about these things tomorrow."

Late in the afternoon, everyone seemed to be gathering around in the foyer. They were talking about how the day was spent and what wonderful art work at the museums and the morning spent at Province Town. Most of them enjoyed the ride over on the ship, "Holiday." It had been a gorgeous day for being outside but now everyone had changed into their party clothes and the big band music had taken over.

Hilda came downstairs and noticed Regis sitting at a small table near the band stand. As she approached, he said, "My, but don't you look rested and so beautiful. Hilda had decided to wear one of her dresses that Lenora had commented about being very classy. Hilda laughed saying, "We have to do some more dancing tonight because tomorrow night on the ship you know what I will probably be doing."

Regis smiled and said, "You will have your child in tow and the Tates will be all over the ship having a great time. They have been looking forward to this trip for over a year. The ship has been in dry dock for repairs and whatever but it is now ready to sail. To them this is the height of society, sailing on the Queen Elizabeth."

Sitting there talking with Regis, Hilda wondered just what kind of agenda would be for her next week. Her mind wondered to other things and started asking Regis about some of the Tate's guests. He told her that all of the guests were wealthy, academic, most were well traveled and lived in beautiful estates. He commented that he had been to several of their homes because the Tates had been invited there for functions. She mentioned the name of the Langleys from Hartford and he said that the Tates were close friends of the Langleys. They go on trips together but they will not be on this trip with them.

Hilda was confused in her mind but she didn't want Regis to have any inkling of what was going on in her mind, so she dropped the subject, saying, "Come on let's dance. The music is too good to sit still."

Regis was up on his feet and had her in his arms before Hilda knew what was happening. She decided that she would just enjoy the evening because she would be in a different world this time tomorrow evening. Hilda felt like a girl at the prom, laughing, talking and telling Regis what a great guy he was on the dance floor. Hilda could tell that Regis was having a great time listening to all the flattery she was feeding him. She wondered after returning from the trip would the Tates keep her on as a nanny for Maxine.

Also, if she stayed around Regis more would she be involved with him emotionally.

Around 8: p.m. Mrs. Tate made an announcement from the band stand. She told everyone to be seated and that the food would be out shortly. Hilda noticed several people dressed like wait people standing in the foreground. Immediately, everyone shuffled to their tables and a wall was pushed back showing several rolling tables of food. The delectable aromas filled both rooms now. The wait people started serving drinks. To Hilda, everyone must have been very thirsty because the wine and champagne flowed like a river. People eventually got to the food, which had been kept hot under heat pans.

Regis said, "I am starved, let's go and get some of that food." Hilda got up following behind him and as she passed the Langleys' table, they said, "Hello."

Mrs. Langley said, "I hope you have a great trip and we hope to see you upon your return."

Hilda said, "Thanks very much and it was so nice meeting both of you. This is such a lovely party."

CHAPTER NINE

Hilda finally joined Regis at the food tables saying, "Sorry, I was side-tracked by the Langleys. They seem like a likeable couple. What have you found that I would like to eat? I see you are piling your plate full."

Regis laughed, "I feel that my eyes are bigger than my stomach and have gotten too much now." Hilda kept looking around the tables and noticed there were lots of fish dishes. She tried the lobster thermidor and some stuffed crabs before leaving for their table,

After she and Regis got settled back at the table, Regis being inquisitive, said, "Wonder why the Langleys were catering to you? Usually, none of the Tates guests are interested in the employees."

Hilda said to Regis, "There could only be one reason and they might think that it is a probability that after the trip I would be in the market for a position. Anyway, that is yet to be decided by the Tates. Who knows after the trip Maxine might not let them get rid of me."

Regis smiling, mumbling, "I am with Maxine. Maybe I should put a bug in her ear before you all sail. Of course, Maxine has a registered nurse on duty at all times which makes me wonder as to who will staying, you or the nurse. I feel like they would not have hired you for the trip if they were going to keep the nurse on duty. Also, I had heard Mrs. Tate say that Maxine needed a person who was a certified teacher. So, I feel that you will be secure in your position as of now."

Hilda looked at Regis, jokingly saying, "You are making me feel important. Really, I think that I would feel at ease working for the Tates. So we'll just have wait and see after the trip. Speaking of the trip, let's dance before the bewitching hour takes over."

Regis and Hilda danced the whole set played by the band. Not too many couples were still around when Hilda said goodnight to Regis.

Hilda started to her room when Mrs. Tate said, "Hilda, we'll get together in the middle of the morning to make sure everything is in order for Regis to pick up our baggage to carry to the ship. I am so excited and I hope you are, too. This trip has been planned for a wonderful vacation. If you have any questions, let me know tomorrow and thank you so much for being here for us."

In her room, Hilda sat down for a moment to get herself together. After talking with Mrs. Tate, she had a good feeling about the trip. Possibly, she would be kept on as Maxine's nanny. At least, she felt that way for now. She really had no qualms about what the next thirty days might hold for her future. From now on, Maxine would be the central figure in her daily routine. Before going to bed, she went to her room and saw she was fast asleep. What a beautiful child, she thought.

The night flew by or it seemed to Hilda as she prepared to go downstairs for breakfast. Maxine had come to the room, said she was hungry. Hilda knew the day would be full of to-do things before the ride to the ship. So off to the dining room with Maxine for breakfast.

As she and Maxine entered the dining room, Mrs. Tate said, "Good morning. This is going to be a beautiful day for all of us. Most of our guests are leaving for home and we'll go about getting ourselves ready for the ride to the ship after lunch. Oh, happy day, I have been looking forward to this trip for sometime."

Hilda wondered why Mrs. Tate was so elated over the trip. Of course, it is going to be a lovely trip but it seemed to her that Mrs. Tate was really going a bit overboard. Maxine and Hilda just sat there relaxed eating their breakfast while Mrs. Tate was talking and sometimes singing.

As Hilda and Maxine were leaving the dining room, Mrs. Tate said, "We'll have all the luggage picked up by Regis right after lunch, so be prepared to go at that time. I am so looking forward to those beautiful suites that I have heard so much about on the

Queen Elizabeth. Hilda, I do hope you enjoy this trip. I know you will be busy with Maxine but an ocean voyage is an incredible way to enjoy a vacation. Sailing on this ship has been a dream of mine for years and it is difficult to believe that it is finally coming true. I wish I could have invited some of my best friends to have accompanied us."

Hilda said, "Mrs. Tate, I know this is going to be a rewarding trip for you and Mr. Tate. You have everything so well planned, so just relax and let everything take its course. Maxine and I will have a great time together and I don't want you to have any worries regarding her. I have lots of things planned for Maxine to do. I will get into some academic things which she will do every day and we'll explore the ship in many ways. So, I want you and Mr. Tate to just relax and have much fun. I will tend to Maxine."

As Mrs. Tate left, Hilda told her that everything was ready for Regis to take charge of her luggage.

Hilda and Maxine left the dining area to go upstairs to rest awhile before leaving for the ship. Hilda knew that it wouldn't be long before Regis showed up to collect her luggage. Also, she noticed when they arrived upstairs that Maxine's luggage had been collected with hers inside her room. She had already been informed that her and Maxine would be sharing a nice suite on the trip. Now a good relaxed feeling possessed Hilda, so her mind was at ease for the moment.

About 2: p.m. Regis knocked on Hilda's bedroom door and as she opened it, Maxine ran outside into the hallway, noisily saying, "I bet we are ready to go."

Hilda smiled as she noticed Regis collecting the luggage. She would miss him for sure but right now she didn't have time for romance. She said, "Drop that stuff and give me a big hug right here so it will be a little more private than on deck of the ship." He smiled from ear to ear, not saying a word, gave her a great big hug, mumbling, "Until your return."

Immediately, he lifted the luggage and was off to the limo. Hilda and Maxine followed behind and as they approached the limo garage, they saw the Tates smiling, waiting for them. Everyone got seated except Mr. Tate who was giving Regis some last minute instructions.

Upon arrival at the dock where the Queen Elizabeth was anchored, people were milling around like an ant bed which had just been disturbed. Mr. Tate took care of everything so all they had to do was let the purser direct them to their suites, which were side by side that was handy for Hilda, in case she ever needed the Tates.

The suites were very large with a small sitting room, a bedroom and bath. They were equipped with everything a person might need, phone, inter-suite communication and personal maid. Hilda reflected upon this type of service, if she were home Jerlene would be there to wait on her. This brought some thought to the letter she had received last week from Jerlene. Jerlene didn't seem like her old self in writing. But, she did mention that her Poppa was doing great, just getting older. I must remember, she thought, to send her some postal cards of the ship's docking as Jerlene has requested.

Straight up 4: p.m. the Queen Elizabeth was on her way. As Hilda was going to be on this ship for thirty days, she opened her luggage and began putting her and Maxine's clothes in a closet in the bedroom. Maxine would talk about the ship and giggle. She would say, "Ms. Hilda, The ship is moving, we are moving." Hilda thought to herself, she is such a precious child but a lonely one.

After emptying the luggage and putting other items in the chest of drawers, Hilda said to Maxine, "Come here and let's talk about what we might be doing on this trip."

"Miss Hilda, I brought a couple of toys that I thought might enjoy the trip, so here they are in this other bag." Hilda didn't notice the bag when unpacking so in opening them she found a large teddy bear and a doll.

Hilda said, "Maxine why did you pick these two friends?"

"Well, Miss Hilda, they are the two that I have always had with me when I was so lonely. I couldn't leave them behind because I didn't want them to feel like I did so many times. It is such a horrible feeling when you are lonely. Mommy and Daddy were always going some where."

Hilda grabbed her real quick saying, "Baby, you and I will not be lonely on this trip, will we?" We will keep busy and Miss Hilda is going to pretend that I am your school teacher. We will be doing some numbers, reading, spelling and drawing."

"Oh, Miss. Hilda, will we really be doing all of them. I love all of them." Big tears filled Hilda's eyes but she immediately wiped them away.

Hilda heard a knock on door of her suite and as she opened the door, the Tates were standing there in full regalia. They informed her that they had been invited to the Captain's Table for dinner and cocktails. Mrs. Tate said, "If you want anything just tell your wait person, or you and Maxine can go to the dining room. These instructions will apply for the whole trip."

Hilda told the Tates to have a good time that they were doing fine. Don't worry about anything, Maxine and I are getting along well and having fun." The Tates left laughing, saying, "We'll see you two sometime tomorrow afternoon.

Next day, Monday, in the morning time, Hilda and Maxine walked around the deck. Lots of people were sunning and lounging in the deck chairs. Hilda found a spot where she and Maxine could see the ocean. Maxine was so involved looking around and admiring the new scenery, then said she was hungry, so Hilda decided they would go to the dining room and have breakfast.

Going back to the suite, Maxine said, "Ms Hilda can we go swimming. I haven't been swimming in a long time." Thinking, Hilda said to herself that she hadn't been in years. So why not but she would have to secure a swimsuit from one of the ship's stores. She already knew that Maxine had one from seeing her nurse pack her bags. Hilda found just what she wanted from a thrift shop on the first floor. Maxine was getting hyper by the minute because she kept saying, "We are going swimming, we are going swimming." Hilda really had not been in much sun in a good while. She definitely did not want to get too much of the sunshine and become ill. Looking around in the shop where she purchased her swimsuit she found some sun screen.

Arriving at the suite, they both got into their swimsuits and grabbed some towels eventhough Hilda knew there would be some at the pool. Then, they were off to the swimming area with Maxine enjoying everything, giggling, and pulling on Hilda's hand. Hilda had a good feeling. She knew Maxine was in seventh heaven today.

While Maxine played in the children's pool, Hilda sat in a chair nearby to observe her. It wasn't too crowded and Maxine was having a ball as she talked with a little boy and girl sitting down in the pool. Hilda watched the sun and moved into the shade not too far from where Maxine was playing in the children's pool. She was glad that she had put loads of sun screen on Maxine because the sun was very intense. Hilda put more sun screen on her own arms and legs. After about forty five minutes, She called Maxine over and looked at her skin. She felt that she had her share of the sun for the day.

Back in the suite, Hilda and Maxine bathed and changed into walking shorts and shirts. Maxine by this time was getting sleepy, so she went into the bedroom. When Hilda checked on her she found her fast asleep.

Hilda could not leave the suite, so she found a couple of books and read awhile. She thought about catching upon her correspondence, so she wrote a few cards to some old friends. She thought, they will be surprised when they get a card from me, saying that I am on the high seas headed for Europe.

Maxine slept like a tired child for about an hour. Hilda wrote many cards to mail at the purser's desk when they left the suite for the dining room to have some refreshments. As yet, the Tates had not shown up anywhere. Hilda thought maybe they had such a grand time at the party, maybe they were still resting in bed.

While eating, Hilda promised Maxine they would get dressed up and go to the lounge for entertainment by the Broadway cast of "Guys and Dolls." A traveling company of the show was performing on the Queen Elizabeth for the whole tour and had been getting great reviews.

As Hilda and Maxine were leaving the dining room, in walked the Tates. Hilda said, "I know you both had a great time last evening. I have promised Maxine I would take her to see the cast of "Guys and Dolls" in the lounge tonight."

Mrs. Tate spoke up quickly, "Yes, you both will enjoy the show, we saw it last evening. Miss Hilda, you carry on just like Maxine is your child. Mr. Tate and I are having so much fun. If you need anything, you know what to do and where I am. We are so blessed to have you with us."

Hilda back in the suite, felt so confused. Mrs. Tate hardly said a word to that child upon seeing her or leaving her. She seems so self-centered, completely ignoring Maxine. She let me know that she was having a ball. There is something that I don't know that is keeping me from putting this jig-saw puzzle together. But, I will keep trying to find out.

After saying good-night to Maxine, she found her book. She read until almost mid-night and it seemed that Maxine was resting well, so she went to bed.

The next day, Hilda vowed to find out more about the relationship between Maxine and her parents. They seemed to love the child, but didn't seem really concerned about her emotional stability, turning the child's complete welfare over to Hilda.

Now, on the fourth day of the ocean crossing to England, Maxine's parents had not been one time to the suite to check on her. Of course, Hilda and Maxine ran into them here and there but they paid little attention to their daughter. Most of the conversation was directed to Hilda, letting her know that they were enjoying the trip. It seemed that Maxine didn't mind them not noticing her. As a matter of fact, she seemed to ignore them in a child like manner. This behavior bothered Hilda because she had been brought up in a loving atmosphere by her Poppa.

Hilda was not worried about the situation with Maxine and her parents because she felt sooner or later that an answer would come forth.

She thought, how wonderfully blessed I am to be employed by wealthy folks, on my way to a month's tour of Europe. Poppa seemed so proud for me as stated in the last letter from him and Jerlene. She wondered if they missed her as much as she missed them. Not only did she miss them but she missed being in D'Lo. She missed the shopping trips to Jackson with Poppa and Jerlene.

Tears came into her eyes, thinking would she ever see D'Lo again. Again, she would say to herself, "I'll worry about that tomorrow."

The phone rang in the suite and as Hilda answered, Mrs. Tate said, "Miss Hilda, you and Maxine meet us in the main dining room at 6: PM." Hilda said, "We'll be there."

Hilda looked at Maxine saying, "We are going to meet your Mom and Dad in the dining room at 6: PM, I suppose to dine with them."

Nonchalantly, Maxine said, "Ok, if that is what they want to do. Do we have to get dressed up?

Hilda said, "Well, maybe we should spruce up a bit, don't you think?"

Maxine threw her arms up in the air, saying, 'Oh, well!"

Hilda thought to herself, "What makes a child have this type of attitude?" She acts as if she is more at ease with me than with her parents. Hilda felt that they would be in England in a couple of days and that she and Maxine would be seeing less and less of them on land. This was the impression Mrs. Tate made when interviewing her for the nanny position, saying, "We will be socializing with friends at their country estates."

When Hilda and Maxine arrived in the dining room, the Tates were already seated at a table. Mrs. Tate asked Hilda if she would like a cocktail before dinner. Hilda ordered a glass of blush wine. Maxine seemed a little restless and Hilda asked her if she would like a soda. Maxine said quickly, "I really would, Miss Hilda." Again, as Hilda noticed, the Tates hardly recognized Maxine being present.

Mr. Tate ordered a magnum of champagne and it was consumed by him and Mrs. Tate before any food was ordered. Hilda enjoyed her glass of blush wine and stated that she needed some food for her and Maxine. Hilda felt that if she didn't mention food that they would keep drinking and talking. So many people kept coming by talking with the Tates, interrupting the dining process, thought Hilda.

Hilda overheard a couple say to the Tates, "You know your little girl favors her mother more and more as she gets older. I was shocked when I heard about the accident." This threw Hilda into a spin because all the time she had been led to believe that Mrs.

Tate was her mother. Were the Tates deliberately trying to keep this information from her? This sort of explained why they were not as attentive to Maxine as real parents would be. Hilda thought to herself, "At the right time, I will talk with Mrs. Tate about Maxine."

After dining Hilda and Maxine stayed in the lounge to watch the evening entertainment. Maxine loved the magician and the dancers but after sitting awhile she became sleepy. Before leaving, the Tates told Hilda that the ship would be docking tomorrow afternoon around 4: PM and everything had been taken care of relative to disembarkation. Everyone was told to meet in the ship's lounge at 3: PM and to make sure that all luggage had been secured in their suite for removal to shore.

Hilda remembered that Mrs. Tate had told her that they would be staying in a hotel in London near Trafalgar Square. She also mentioned as Hilda remembered that she and Mr. Tate were invited to several parties while in London. Of course, this meant that her and Maxine would be spending lots of time together.

Maxine had fallen asleep and as she was aroused by Hilda, Mrs. Tate said, "She gets sleepy so easily."

Hilda smiled, saying, "Mrs. Tate would you stop by the suite in the morning. I need to ask you about some details before leaving the ship."

Mrs. Tate replied, "In the morning, I will see you."

It seemed to Hilda that the night went by in a flash because after securing everything in their luggage for preparation on leaving the ship the next day, she fell into bed exhausted.

As promised, Mrs. Tate knocked on her door the next morning and as she approached she began looking around the suite. Hilda, not really caring what Mrs. Tate might think said, "Maxine and I are ready to disembark. I believe Maxine is ready to see land for a change as she seems to have some restless periods during the day which I can understand for a child of her age."

CHAPTER TEN

Mrs. Tate said, "I will say again that Mr. Tate and I are very fortunate to have found you. Maxine does have some behavioral problems but you seem to know how to handle them."

Quickly, Hilda felt that this was the right time to confront Mrs. Tate regarding Maxine. Hilda said, Mrs. Tate do you have a few minutes while Maxine is busy playing with the toy she brought on trip? I know that you haven't discussed Maxine very much with me, so I would like to ask a few questions about her. Last night, a lady approached you at dinner and I overheard her say, "Your daughter looks more and more like her Mother. So sorry to hear about the accident."

Mrs. Tate was completely stunned, hearing Hilda ask these questions. She got her second breath and almost choked up as she said, "Maxine belongs to a friend of mine that was killed instantly in a very bad auto accident. Her father was incapacitated from the accident and therefore he asked me to take her as my child. Really, I was hesitant in accepting this responsibility because as you see my husband and I are always on the go. My husband did not want me to adopt Maxine and under these circumstances it has been difficult for me to be close to her. I am sure you have noticed that we are not real close like mother and daughter should be. I try to be close to Maxine but I am so much involved in other things. That is why we are so glad to have you with us."

Hilda shook her head for a moment and then she said, "Mrs. Tate, I will not always be around and one day Maxine is going to an adult. I am not going to tell you how to run your life. But if you don't try to be close and show her some affection, it is going to effect her whole life. You surely don't want her to hate you. She is such a dear child and so smart."

Mrs. Tate, as Hilda could observe, by now had tears in her eyes. She bent her head over in her lap and started crying. She started to speak but was so full of emotion that she couldn't. Hilda put her arms around her shoulders and patted her back until she could compose herself.

It was a quiet time until Mrs. Tate stood up and said, "I am so glad that you now understand the situation. Maybe if she was really my flesh and blood, things would be different but I have a husband who thinks different. My husband comes first and that is the problem I must face everyday. I hope that you will plan to stay with us for a long time because Maxine and you get along so well together.

Hilda said, "When I was interviewed for the position, you and Mr. Tate told me that I would be employed for the length of your vacation cruise. Are you now saying something different? Anyway, I know you have to meet with your husband to prepare for disembarkation proceedings, so we can talk more about this at the end of the cruise. Maxine is getting restless with her toy so I will spend sometime with her before we get ourselves together.

To Hilda, it seemed that Mrs. Tate was glad to get away quickly. She didn't say one word to Maxine as she immediately left the suite. Hilda felt better having the talk with Mrs. Tate. She might really want to get rid of me when we return from the cruise, was uppermost in Hilda's mind. She really didn't care because it might be best for Maxine to spend more time with Mrs. Tate.

While in deep thought waiting in the suite, a knock on the door and there were the valets to get the luggage. After they retrieved the luggage, Hilda picked up her purse and got Maxine by the hand to walk to the ship's lounge, where everyone was suppose to congregate until getting off the ship.

Sitting in the lounge, Hilda noticed all the passengers. Easily, you could tell all had money or could easily get it. She said to herself, "I must write Jerlene a long letter telling her and Poppa about everything." Hilda thought, I have been gone almost six months and I really miss the little town of D'Lo. I hope Jerlene is taking care of my Poppa. Poppa has been so good to me especially sending that New York bank a $2,500 deposit for me.

The purser came out and announced the way to exit off the ship. Hilda stood up and holding Maxine's hand walked toward the opening. When they got off the ship, Mr. and Mrs. Tate was waiting with a taxi. As they drove through London toward the hotel, Hilda thought, this is one beautiful place. She was so glad that it was daylight so she could observe everything. Maxine's little eyes were lit up like a Christmas tree. Hilda thought, I don't understand why anyone could not love this sweet, little girl.

When they arrived at the Hotel Clarion near Trafalgar Square, and as the Tate's entered the lobby, several people came toward them. There was much hugging and talking. Hilda surmised that they were old friends of the Tate's.

After all the greetings, Mrs. Tate told the bellboy to take Hilda to her suite. She and Maxine followed him to the elevator. Hilda couldn't behold the splendor of the accommodations provided for her and Maxine. Upon their arrival, their luggage was already in place.

Not long after Hilda and Maxine were situated in their suite, the room phone rang. It was Mrs. Tate, asking Hilda to meet them for dinner in dress-up attire. Hilda thought that might be a bit of a problem, the clothes being pressed by the luggage, but, she told Mrs. Tate she would be in the lobby at the appropriate time.

After dressing for dinner, Hilda and Maxine sat down for awhile before meeting with the Tates. Hilda could tell Maxine was full of wanting to ask about this and that. She told her when they came back from dinner, she would answer all of her questions. Maxine smiled and said it would be much fun. Hilda could tell that Maxine was not too enthused about eating with the Tates even though she had menioned earlier that she was hungry.

As Hilda and Maxine left the suite to meet the Tates, Maxine said, "Do we have to stay very long? I'm tired." Hilda commented, "Just as soon as we get through eating we'll see about leaving. I am a little tired myself.""

On the way down, Hilda noticed that Maxine seemed agog over everything, especially after they entered the lobby from the elevator. She will be bubbling over with questions when we return, Hilda thought, if she doesn't fall asleep.

The Tates were waiting for them when they approached the dining area. Again, there was much hugging and greetings from those who were old friends of the Tates. The Tates had traveled extensively and had made many friends, some were folks from back home who had come along on this trip.

Of course, Hilda didn't care who they really were at this stage of the game. She did notice that she had been introduced to several couples at the party the day before sailing, and made it a point to see if the Langleys from Hartford, Connecticut were in attendance. This couple, as someone mentioned during the evening, didn't come on the cruise. Again, even in the crowd, Hilda thought of her baby with much anticipation.

As soon as Maxine was through eating, Hilda whispered to her, saying, "I have eaten enough. Are you ready to go?" Maxine eyes lit up, and she squeezed Hilda's hand.

She told Mrs. Tate, "Maxine is getting sleepy, So we are retiring for the evening."

Mr. and Mrs. Tate smiled at Hilda as they left the party and Mrs. Tate whispered she would see her in the morning about the day's agenda. As Hilda and Maxine maneuvered through the crowd, several noticed Maxine and commented, "What a beautiful child!"

Arriving at the elevator, Maxine already had started asking questions. Hilda thought, I must be careful how I answer these questions because she might relay answers to someone else. I don't want her to be critical of others. As they entered the suite, Maxine sat down on a couch beside Hilda. After a few more questions, she was very sleepy and Hilda handed her a gown. By the time she'd changed, she ran to one of the beds in the suite and fell upon it, saying, "Goodnight, Miss Hilda." Hilda bent over, gave her a hug, and pulled the cover around her.

Lying in bed, Hilda thought about the days ahead, hoping that her and Maxine would be able to take a few tours and see some of the points of interest. Maybe that is what Mrs. Tate will tell her about tomorrow. Actually, the main thing in her mind was what would happen when they returned to Boston in four weeks. Poppa and Jerlene popped in and out of her thoughts as she tried to go to sleep.

About 9: a.m. the next morning, Mrs. Tate made her appearance and asked Hilda to sit down to go over the schedule while in London. Hilda noticed most of the next week or so would be in London. Mrs. Tate told her that they would be visiting in friends' country estates and would probably be gone for a week. She gave Hilda a purse with money so the two girls could could entertain themselves while they were gone, When Hilda counted the money, she found a thousand dollars in bills.As she said, "Goodby," Mrs. Tate was all giggles, and even hugged Maxine as she went out the door.

Hilda was stunned a bit, but in a way, also saddened because Mrs. Tate didn't say anything about checking on them during the week. Of course, there were phone numbers where they could be reached. Hilda thought, "Maxine and I will have a good time looking this place over the next few days, but today we stay within walking distance of the hotel."

That afternoon, She and Maxine took short walks around the hotel area. She inquired about tours at the hotel desk information and finally lined up four differnt tours for the next 4 days. They had all their meals served in their suite, and enjoyed themselves immensely.

Days went by, and Hilda and Maxine enjoyed themselves. On the eighth day, Mrs. Tate called to say that she would be by to see them but they would be going on to Paris with some friends and they were to stay put in the hotel until their return. Hilda was not surprised over the call but if they were going to be gone longer they would need more money. Anyway, she would see what Mrs. Tate had to say when she stopped by.

Not too long after Mrs. Tate's call, Hilda heard a knock and the door opened. There stood Mrs. Tate dressed to kill as they say in the South. Hilda told her she looked good and Mrs. Tate beamed.

She said, "Miss Hilda, I have really been having a grand time and it is mostly because of you. Here is some more money. I know you will need it. Traveling is expensive and so is this place. You all enjoy yourselves and eat well. She, again hugged Maxine before leaving, which pleased Hilda.

When she looked into the money bag which Mrs. Tate had left. There was a note saying, "Go shopping. Buy something you have always wanted. Have fun." Hilda counted the money which was $5000 in bills, she thought, "This is her way of compensating for time not spent with her child." Well, she and Maxine would live it up in London, maybe see one of those English musicals, which they try to copy from us."

Things rocked on, Hilda and Maxine went out almost every day and within a week they were very familiar with London town. They were having a great time just being together. Maxine had completely let herself go and was more talkative with Hilda. She had learned some of the melodies they had heard in some of the musicals they had attended.

But a week had gone by and no word from the Tates. On the tenth day, as they were getting ready for bed, the telephone rang. It was Mrs. Tate inquiring if all was ok. Hilda told her they'd been having a great time and now knew a lot about London. Mrs. Tate told Hilda they were now headed for Italy with some friends and for her to contact the information desk of the hotel because she had wired her more money. Mrs. Tate kept her on the phone explaining what a great time they had been having with their friends.

After hanging up the phone, Hilda was beside herself. She could not understand how a mother could be so cold toward her child, especially such a sweet child as Maxine. She explained to Maxine that her mother had called but Maxine didn't seem to care one way or the other.

One thing Hilda couldn't seem to understand was when interviewed for this position she was not told exactly her duties would be. She was under the impression she would be going along with the Tates from country to country not holding up in a hotel in London while the couple jumped from country to country with friends. Anyway, she had enjoyed being in London with Maxine. Probably, upon their return from wherever, the Tates would be back in London to return on the ship back to Boston.

Hilda and Maxine ate every meal out in some nice restaurant every day. They had been shopping and found some new dresses for Maxine. Several toys had been found to suit Maxine's fancy. She was a happy child around Hilda but when talking about going back home, she became a different child. Hilda was hoping she would talk more about her life before she became her Nanny but for some reason it didn't happen.

It had been about eight days since hearing from Mrs. Tate and as Hilda and Maxine was returning to the hotel after an outing, that the hotel desk called her over. She had a wire from the Tates saying that they would be in touch with her soon. They had sent a phone number if Hilda needed to contact them.

Hilda didn't think much about the situation, so everything rocked on for another week or so. Coming into the hotel lobby, after spending the day at the White Cliffs of Dover, the Tates approached them. They were both tan from being on the beach. Both hugged Hilda and Maxine while telling them what a wonderful time they'd been having on their trips.

The Tates asked Hilda to meet them for dinner in the main restaurant because they wanted to discuss the trip back home. Hilda was confused a bit because she didn't realize it was time to return back to Boston.

Hilda had enjoyed the trip to London and in a way was glad to be thinking about the return trip. She had to make up her mind what would be best for her relative to her position with the Tates or moving on to get closer to her baby Gloria.

The dinner with the Tates was very enjoyable and Maxine seemed to be talkative as Mrs. Tate questioned her about what they had been doing and seeing. She let her know right away that she had enjoyed being with Miss Hilda.

Mrs. Tate did all the talking with Mr. Tate listening. She outlined the return trip being within two days and said to have bags packed for pickup in the morning by the hotel valet.

This has been an eye-opening trip for me, Hilda thought. I've have never seen such a self-centered person as Mrs. Tate. She will never get the attention of Maxine until she becomes more aware of her. This made Hilda think more about her position. She would love to be able to move on maybe find a nanny job in Hartford which is between New York and Boston. As usual, when not thinking straight, she said, "I'll think about it tomorrow."

The next couple of days flew by and all went well getting back on the ship to return home. The sailing back home was restful and much dining was done with the Tates. They both seemed to be more settled down after getting all the social whirl out of their system. In the evening there was much entertainment on the ship and Hilda and Maxine were invited to participate with Tates. Maxine enjoyed much of the early evening but would get sleepy and Hilda would leave to put her to bed. Mrs. Tate offered to get a sitter from the ship's office for Maxine if Hilda wanted to stay and enjoy the entertainment. Hilda refused the offer, indicating that she had rather stay with Maxine for now.

The Tates were very pleased with Hilda's performance and had been talking among themselves, hoping they could persuade her to remain as Maxine's nanny. The Tates felt they had found a jewel, and upon arrival back home, had planned to have a talk with Hilda about taking on all the duties of the household. The Tates felt that Hilda was a very responsible person who could manage something.

The last night before leaving the ship, Hilda caught up on her correspondence. She wrote Poppa and Jerlene a long, newsy letter. She knew that when she got back to the Tate's home, there would be mail from them. She could hardly wait to find out what was going on in D'Lo. Giggling a bit, she thought, if some of these people could see the little town where I came from, they probably would be horrified. I miss it so much sometime and then, maybe it was good for me to get away for awhile. Hilda always carried the idea with her that some day she would be back in her beloved D'Lo.

Leaving the ship was easier than getting on because Regis was there to help. Hand in hand, Hilda and Maxine walked down the steps to the dock behind the Tates. Regis had spotted them and was waving and they waved back. As he retrieved their baggage and directed them to the limo, he chattered away. He seemed so glad to see everyone. He hugged them all except Mr. Tate.

As they rode through Boston, Hilda noticed how beautiful the weather was at the beginning of early fall. In her mind, she tried to compare the weather with the weather back in D'Lo. It would not be long before real cool weather would take over and she wondered if she would like it or not.

Arriving at the Tate complex, Hilda noticed that everything was clean, grounds were freshly cut, and the employees were in clean uniforms.

Regis got Hilda and Maxine settled back in their rooms and as Hilda sat down, she realized that she was a little tired. As Regis left, he told Hilda that he wanted to talk with her later. Hilda nodded okay, but wondered why.

She got Maxine ready for bed because she had fallen asleep in her room not long after getting settled back in her routine. Being seven years of age, Hilda wondered if she really enjoyed being away from home these past four weeks. Hilda thought to herself that she felt tired and she could easily see, so was Maxine by the way she acted the last couple of days. She was hoping that she would bounce back in a few days.

Hilda sat in her suite wondering why Regis was so adamant in wanting to converse with her. Before retiring, Mrs. Tate knocked on her door and wanted to if they needed anything. In leaving, she asked Hilda to be available in the morning after breakfast so they could have a little chat. Hilda informed her that she would only be unpacking her and Maxine's luggage from the trip.

After Mrs Tate left, the phone rang and it was Regis asking if he could talk with her for a moment. Hilda told him that he could come to her suite or she could meet him downstairs.

He paused for a moment on the phone saying, "Why don't I take you and Maxine for a drive in the morning?"

Hilda said, "I think that would be a great idea after I have a short conference with Mrs. Tate after breakfast."

Regis said, "That will be splendid, see you then."

As Hilda went to bed, she was still curious why Regis was so anxious to talk with her. As usual, she said to herself, "I'll worry about that tomorrow."

The whole neighborhood was awakened next morning with the sound of sirens. There was a big fire in a home about two blocks from the Tate Complex. As Hilda and Maxine proceeded downstairs for breakfast, everyone was running around, in and out, trying to see what was going on.

Finally, after settling down Hilda and Maxine had a big breakfast. Maxine seemed to be more herself today and Hilda was glad. She talked quite a bit about the ship and walking through the squares in London. Hilda knew that soon she would be asking questions about lots of things she had encountered on the trip.

As Hilda and Maxine left the dining room, Mrs. Tate asked Hilda if she would take Maxine up to her playroom so they could have a chat. Hilda did as Mrs. Tate requested and returned to Mrs. Tate's office.

As Hilda entered the office on the first floor of the Tate's main house, Mrs. Tate was sitting waiting for her. Hilda noticed as she sat down that Mrs. Tate's expression was of a serious nature. She seemed restless as she started to talk, saying, "Hilda, I am at a loss of how to begin telling you of my problem. But Mr. Tate and I are having marital differences and it seems that it had started before we left on our trip. I am planning to go away for awhile until things can be more settled. I can't really say how long it will be, but Mr. Tate and I want you to stay on as nanny for Maxine. Your salary will be doubled if you stay, and Regis will be at your disposal when needed." Mr. Tate has assured me of this situation."

Hilda was not expecting a situation of this type to enter into her life but here it was, so she had to make a decision. Hilda said, "Mrs. Tate do you have any idea how long you will be away? Mrs. Tate looked straight into her face, with tears in her eyes, saying, "Hilda, it wont be long, I hope." Hilda came back saying, "Will I be able to contact you without any trouble? What if something happens to Maxine?" Mrs. Tate replied, "Yes, I will leave a number and address where I will be at your beck and call. If you need anything while I am gone you only have to ask Mr. Tate."

Hilda thought to herself, "Well, I am really not going anywhere right now, so I may as well just stay here for awhile and see what happens." She got up from her chair and walked over to Mrs. Tate and hugged her saying, "For now, I will stay around."

Mrs. Tate broke down and cried so profusely that Hilda could hardly understand her saying, "Thanks so much, Maxine loves you and we do, too. You have been a blessing to us all."

As Hilda left, she ran into Regis in the hallway and she said to him, "When do we take our ride? Smiling, he said, "Right now, if you are ready, meet me at the limo in just a few minutes."

CHAPTER ELEVEN

Outside, holding Maxine's hand, waiting for Regis, Hilda was approached by Mr. Tate saying, "Mrs. Tate said that she has spoken with you and that you have agreed to stay with us. Well, if you need anything just let me know. I will be in and out of the complex every day and thank you. Regis knows where I am at all times."

As he left, Regis backed out of the garage, stopped and jumped out to open the limo doors. Regis said, "Let Maxine sit on the back seat as the doors will be locked and you sit up front with me so I can talk with you."

Hilda obeyed and seated herself in the front with Regis. She turned around to make sure that Maxine was secure and happy. Maxine was laughing and fondling her old dog toy that she liked so well. She seemed to like toy animals better that dolls.

The morning was beautiful, plenty of sunshine and clear skies. Hilda waited as they drove along to see what Regis would say. Finally, he said, "Let's stop at a beautiful park that I go to sometime. We can get out and sit on the benches and have something to drink. I am sure Maxine would love that. Hilda nodded her head in approval.

Arriving at the park, Hilda thought of the D'Lo rocks where she would go on picnics with friends. The river running by reminded her of Strong River so much and she had a feeling of homesickness. Before she made the decision stay, maybe she should have made a short trip home to see Poppa and Jerlene.

Regis noticed that, she seemed to be lost in thought, aroused her to reality by saying, "Let's sit over here on this big bench and talk."

Hilda retorted. "Just what do you want to talk to me about?"

Regis said, "Have you heard anything about the split between Mr. and Mrs. Tate? Much gossip has abounded between some of their friends, while they were gone, that they were having marital troubles. Is this going to effect you in any way?"

Hilda smiled saying, "Regis, they have asked me to stay while Mrs. Tate is away and that you will be at my beck and call. I really don't know how long this will last or how long she will be gone as I could not find out.Do you know just what the trouble is between Mr. and Mrs. Tate? Sometimes people with money seem to have more trouble than those who are less fortunate." She thought, I always had a man to take care of the money problems, my Poppa. Bless his soul, I love him dearly. I hope Jerlene is taking good care of him.

Regis seemed a bit overjoyed saying, "I was hoping that you would be around. The gossip around is that Mr. Tate has been financing another woman across town who happens to be a long time friend of Mrs. Tate. Another friend of Mrs Tate told her about it a week before they left on the trip. She confronted Mr. Tate, so I am told, and he confessed to it but told Mrs. Tate that he only loaned her the money for a payment on a condo on the Eastside which is a very affluent neighborhood. Mrs. Tate's friend, who lives nearby, told her that she had seen Mr. Tate within the neighborhood. In reality, this could be a complete breakup, divorce and all, if it is not handled properly by both sides. I know both of them very well and both are stubborn. Both of them are well off, because both of them have money. I won't say they got it honest because that is another story. You don't need to worry you pretty head about all this stuff anyway."

Hilda said, "We'll see how everything works out and after awhile if I decide to move on, I will do. I'll miss having you to talk to if I do. You know I really missed you on that trip which Maxine and I didn't really enjoy. We had our good days especially when sightseeing."

Upon arrival back to the compound, they were met by Mr. Tate who told them that their cooperation would be appreciated. He told Hilda that if he was ever needed, to contact Regis because he was in contact with him daily. Mr. Tate had put a woman over the running of the household employees but supervised by Regis, so Hilda could continue what she had been doing. All arrangements met with Hilda's approval.

After Mr. Tate left them, Hilda said, "Regis, you are becoming very important around here. I hope they gave you a good raise in pay, because I feel like you are going to be busy with running this compound."

With a big grin, Regis replied, "Of course, you are your own boss pertaining to your position. But, when I ask you out for an evening or a drive, then I will be your boss. Yes, the Tates have been very generous relative to my salary. I really hate to see them unhappy but it is much worse than you know. There are other differences between the Tates that were not resolved before this one occurred. This one may be the one that broke the camel's back. But anyway, you have enough to think about caring for Maxine."

Hilda gave a deep look at Regis, saying, "Since I have been here these several months, no one has mentioned what Mr. Tate does every day when he leaves the compound. Does he have an office elsewhere? Just how he spent his time? Do you know, and if you do, why haven't you told me?"

Regis' expression shocked Hilda, "Well, honestly I didn't want to worry you about anything other than taking care of Maxine. If you knew what I know about the Tates, you probably would want to leave, but the situation as it exists will not hurt you. What they do is their business and really there is no reason to discuss the whole matter. Some day I will tell you a few things about this family. I only hope, if they do sever their relationship, that some items will not become public information. So for now, don't you worry your pretty little head."

Hilda was busy with Maxine for several weeks and was beginning to wonder why everything was at ease around the complex. Regis had been very attentive to her and Maxine. Mr. Tate was seen around the complex several times but no word from Mrs. Tate. The household had been in a capable person's hands, taken over by Mrs. Styne, and everything was handled in a proper fashion. Matter of fact, Hilda thought that everything from meals to supervision of the employees had been done better than before. Mrs. Styne did take up some time with Maxine when we were around and several times she had come upstairs to check on her. She had told Hilda that when she was needed to let her know.

Even though she had not heard from Mrs. Tate, Hilda had thought about taking a short visit to D'Lo to check on Poppa and Jerlene. It was getting near the Christmas holidays and maybe a week down South would help. She thought about asking Mr. Tate if she could do that at this time and if Mrs. Styne could look after Maxine while she was away.

At supper time, Hilda thought this would be a good time to approach Mr. Tate which she did. While sitting at her table with Regis, Mr. Tate was preparing to leave the dining room when she waved her hand for him to come over. Regis got up to leave as Mr. Tate approached but Hilda said, "Regis, would you stay for a moment. I have something to discuss with you and Mr. Tate."

Both Mr. Tate and Regis looked surprised as Hilda said, "I need about a week off to go to Mississippi to check on my father before the holidays. I have not heard anything from Mrs. Tate about when she will return and I don't suppose you have either, Mr. Tate, or else you would have consulted with me. I asked Mrs. Styne if she would be able to look after Maxine while I'm away and she informed me that she would be glad to do so. So, if that meets with your approval, I would like to be away for a week. I would like for Regis to carry me to New York so I can catch the train direct to Meridian. My father will pick me up there to carry me to my home in D'Lo. He will be beside himself when I let him know I am coming. I need to do this today so he will meet me on Saturday."

Mr. Tate's expression was a sign of grief but he said, "Hilda, I know that you need a break and going home for awhile might be just the change you need because I know you have been very loyal in your position. Yes, Regis may drive you to New York for you to board the train so you will not have to change trains. Make your plans and talk with Mrs. Styne about your trip so everything will be covered while you are gone. Also, stop by the office and I will pay for you trip home. At this time, you are a valuable employee for our household and we appreciate what you are doing, so don't be gone too long."

Hilda in a way felt badly leaving at this time but in her heart she had a feeling that she needed a break from everything, after all it had been almost two years since she saw her Poppa. She commented, "Mr. Tate, I thank you for your consent and I want be gone but a few days. Today is Wednesday, so I will plan for Regis to take me to New York tomorrow evening so I can catch the train at 9: am Friday to Meridian and I should be home by midday Saturday."

Regis seemed dumfounded when he got up to leave and he gave Hilda a stare, saying, "I have something to check out and then I will be with you shortly. Hilda shook her head in approval. Mr. Tate took her hand and said, "Go ahead and get everything worked out. We do appreciate you. By the way, I, too, haven't heard from my wife."

Going up to her room, Hilda, heard someone whistle from the hallway and it was Regis. He said, "Can I have a few words with you in private."

Hilda smiled, "You know that you can anytime you need me. I could tell by your expression that you were at a loss when I asked Mr. Tate about going home for a visit. As far as I know, I will be back when I told Mr. Tate. I am not running off, you know. Anyway, you wouldn't miss me as much as I would miss you. Really, you are like sunshine around this complex, especially the way things are at this time."

Regis came up to her and put his arm around her waist and they walked together to check on Maxine. Maxine was sleeping as usual in the afternoon. As they peeked in on her, Hilda said, "I need to phone my Poppa and Jerlene so he will know to pick me up on Saturday in Meridian."

Regis smiled at her saying, "Let's call right now and see how everything is in Mississippi. If Maxine awakens Mrs. Styne will take care of her while you are on the phone."

Giggly, Hilda made haste to her phone in the room, ringing the number in D'Lo. Jerlene came on the line, saying, "Hello, this is the Webbers residence.

Hilda said, "Jerlene how are you and Poppa." Jerlene replied quickly, "This you Miss Hilda?"

Hilda said, "Jerlene, it's me and is Poppa there."

Pausing, Jerlene said, "Miss Hilda, it is so good to hear your voice, wait a moment, he's out in the backyard."

Hilda said to Regis, "Jerlene has gone to fetch Poppa from the back yard. He must be doing alright if he is out in the yard. Of course, I haven't spoken to him in awhile."

While holding, she heard a voice and she said, Poppa is this you, you don't sound like yourself, are you doing alright?

Replying, he said, I suppose I am doing ok but I have been a little under the weather as we have had some very wet weather. Baby, are you having a good time?"

Quickly she replied, "Poppa can you meet me in Merdian on Saturday somewhere around noon? I am coming home for a visit. I want to see you and Jerlene so bad."

"Yes, baby, nothing can stop me from being in Meridian Saturday, just you be there. Poppa wants to see and talk with you. "Hilda said, "Ok, Poppa, I will see you then."

Regis could tell that she was in a much happier mood after talking with her Poppa. Hilda commented that she would like to leave tomorrow afternoon late and try to call Lenora upon arriving in New York. The last time she conversed with Lenora she could not understand her very well which made her think maybe she been drinking too much. Maybe both her and Regis could spend the night at her apartment. Regis had already agreed to get her to Grand Central Station to catch the train at 9: am Friday.

Regis agreed to what she had planned and commented that everything would be on go but she would have to agree to have dinner at some nice restaurant Thursday night before he returned.

To Hilda, this sounded like a great idea and said that she was looking forward to the evening with a good looking man. But, she needed to start packing her bag for her trip home.

Regis said, Let's get Maxine and go for a short drive down the main boulevard." Hilda shaking her head in approval, went to check on Maxine and she was up playing with her toy dog as usual.

Driving along the boulevard, Hilda noticed the cool weather was turning the foliage to many colors. The weather was beginning to have a cold nip especially in the afternoon. Would she like living in this cold climate? Maybe the trip back to D'Lo would answer some questions flying around in her mind like the cold weather, getting involved emotionally with Regis or moving on.

Driving back to the complex, Hilda said, "Regis, I am going to be a busy woman tonight packing a bag for the trip, so will you let me know when dinner will be served and we'll have a chat while we eat. Regis looked so pleased at Hilda saying, "You bet and woman, I am going to miss you next week."

Leaving Regis at the complex garage, Hilda and Maxine proceeded to their rooms. Upon arriving, Hilda said, "Maxine, Miss Hilda needs to talk with you a moment." Looking up at her, Maxine had tears in her eyes, saying, "Miss Hilda, you will be back, won't you?"

Hilda was at a loss for words, bending down she gathered Maxine in her arms, saying, "Yes, darling, Miss Hilda will be back in a few days. Mrs. Styne will take good care of you while I am away. You like Mrs. Styne because you mentioned that to me the other day. I am going to see my Dad, whom I call Poppa. I am still his little girl, too. I will be so glad to see him and he told me over the phone that he wanted to see me. He loves me, just like I love you." Maxine said, "Miss Hilda, I love you, too."

Maxine hung around Hilda as she packed her bag for the trip home. Hilda felt sorry for her knowing she would be sad until she returned. But, she had not been home since she left almost two years ago.

The next day Hilda tried to be with Maxine as much as possible before Regis picked her up for the drive to New York. About 3: PM, Regis knocked on her door and as she opened the door Maxine was hugging her legs. She noticed tears in Maxine's eyes and Regis said, "Honey, she will be back to be with me and you. She wants to go see her Daddy. It will only be for a few days."

Hilda picked her up and hugged her real tight before leaving. She was touched by her mournful expression of rejection. As they proceeded downstairs to the garage, Mrs. Styne came out and took Maxine by the hand. They were standing side by side as Regis and Hilda pulled out on the street, waving good-by.

Out on the highway toward New York, silence had taken over. The mood of meditation seemed to have conquered all. The day was crisp but sunny and you could easily tell that old man winter was on his way.

Driving along, Regis slipped his right hand into Hilda's lying on the seat beside him. Both turned around to look at each other with smiles that both understood. Regis said, "So you want to call up your friend, Lenora in New York when we arrive? Instead, why don't we just go by and see her? Have you heard from her lately?"

Hilda smiled saying, "I called her on the phone but couldn't understand everything she said which made we think she had been drinking. I think it would be ok for us to drop in on her. Of course, you never know what to expect. Let's just do it anyway, we can always get a hotel room."

Time had passed fast as Regis noticed because they were now in uptown New York, not too far from the Tavern on the Green. As they passed it, Hilda said, "Lenora loved that place and her friend dropped us off there several times when I first came to the big city. His apartment is not too far away."

Regis said, "I know because I checked the address that you gave me when I first picked you up nine months. I am familiar with this section of the city, so we should be there in a short while."

As they drove along, Hilda noticed the familiarity of the streets and knew they were getting closer to Lenora's apartment. As Regis pulled up to the location where he had first seen Hilda, he remembered saying to himself, "What a beautiful lady." Now, he knew she was more than a beautiful lady.

As Regis stopped the limo, he jumped out and opened the door for Hilda. Both of them proceeded up the steps to Lenora's door. Hilda knocked on the apartment door, nothing happened for a short while, then she knocked again. On the second knock the door seemed to be ajar, so Regis pushed it open a bit so they could see inside. As they peered in, the place was empty and while peering in, someone behind them said, "Could I help you folks? Are you looking for an apartment?"

Hilda and Regis both were startled on hearing a voice. Hilda said, "I was looking for a friend, Lenora, who use to live here. The man said, "That young lady was moved out several weeks ago by a man who has a taxi. I didn't get an address of where they were going but I think it was in Brooklyn."

As Hilda and Regis left, they thanked the man for the information. Getting seated back in the limo, not another word was mentioned about Lenora. Regis said, "I think the first thing for us to do is to secure a hotel room so that you can get some rest and remember you promised to go out with me to a very nice restaurant this evening. This is my present for you before going home on your trip."

Hilda commented quickly, "Yes, I will need a place to sleep and refresh myself before I get on that train tomorrow morning. If you will promise to be a good boy, we can obtain a room with two beds if you think that will be satisfactory. Regis smiled, saying, "Whatever you say, I'm with you. The Hotel New Yorker is nearby and I have stayed there before when I was down with the Tates. Also, it is not too far from Grand Central Station where you will board the train."

Hilda said, "I trust your judgment, so let's do it. Also, I am hungry already but I will be more so after I get prepared for the evening. I hope you are going to take me to some place where we can dance. You are a good dancer, do you know that?"

Regis' face lit up saying, "Don't you worry yourself one bit, I have the right place picked out for us to spend a fabulous evening. I have been there with the Tates and the music was just right for ballroom dancing and the food is superb. I even brought me a different suit to wear. I want us to have a great evening."

Hilda, dumfounded, was at a lost for words, but she finally came out with, "A special suit for the occasion. I can't believe all this pre-planning went on but we'll find out later how things turn out, won't we?"

As the limo pulled in at the New Yorker Hotel, More than one valet bounced out to greet them, probably thinking it was some big shot and his girl friend. Of course, Regis was used to that being with the Tates. He told the valet that he would be using the limo later but to go ahead and remove their luggage.

Inside the hotel, Regis went to claim his reservation. Hilda said, "So you made reservations? He smiled, "Yes, I knew that I would have to stay somewhere so I could carry you in style to the train station Friday morning. It is a huge suite, usually, used by the Tates and Mr. Tate gave me permission to handle it this way. He gave me orders to bring you to New York, wine and dine before you left for home and purchase your round trip ticket at his expense. Even though he is a scoundrel, he has a good streak. You see, I am suppose to pick you up at Grand Central Station upon your return. So you will have to let me know when that is."

Hilda was very surprised about everything but glad all the details were handled. She and Regis followed the bellboy up to the suite and found it was actually three or four rooms. She peered around and noticed that it had two separate bedrooms which pleased her very much. She didn't want people at the hotel, even though they didn't know her, to think she was some kind of woman for hire.

She noticed after the valet left that Regis had his luggage in one of the bedrooms, and had hung up his suit. She decided she would do the same with her dress that she planned to wear.

Hilda thought, this must be an expensive suite. It made her wonder about the Tates, they must be very wealthy or getting money from somewhere. Maybe one day Regis will tell me more about our employer and his spouse. Hilda said as usual, "Something's funny about the whole situation but I'll worry about that tomorrow."

She hollered across the room to Regis, "I am going to take a good bath and lay down for a few minutes before our date."

Regis reiterated quickly, "Good idea and I'll do the same. The time is about 4:15 PM, so I will see you after awhile."

A lull over the suite as they got ready to take siestas in separate rooms. Funny, both got their baths, lay down and fell asleep as if they were completely exhausted.

Hilda woke up first and when she looked at the night stand near the bed, the small clock read, 7: p.m. She jumped up, grabbed her robe, and rushed out of the room saying, "Regis, don't you think we should be getting ready for our night on the town?"

He stumbled out of his bedroom, "Boy, that was a great nap. I'm ready for the evening."

They both finished dressing and when Hilda appeared from her room, she was whirling around the room saying, "I feel like dancing all night."

Regis said, "Well, we'll see about that but first I need a good meal. I hope you are hungry because Delmonico's is famous for food and good music.

On the elevator to the hotel lobby, Regis commented, "We will leave the limo put and take the taxi as it's only a couple of blocks from the hotel. First, we'll go by the train station and pick up those reserved tickets, thanks to Mr. Tate, so we want have to worry about that tomorrow morning when I see you off. I dread driving back to Boston all alone tomorrow afternoon. Maybe you won't be gone more than a week."

Hilda smiled, "I don't anticipate staying any longer. Anyway you can call and check on me if you want."

"You know just how to hurt a fellow," chimed Regis, smiling from ear to ear.

Hilda quickly said, "I am getting hungry. Let's go to the station, and then we get settled down to a wonderful evening. You can tell me your life story."

Getting a taxi was easy because as they were approaching the lobby from the elevator a valet approached them, saying, "May I help you?" Regis let him know that he wanted a taxi. He directed them to one parked in the front of the hotel and they were off to the train station.

As the taxi drove up to the parking area of the train station, he informed the driver to wait that he would only be a few minutes and then they would be going to Delmonico's. The taxi driver seemed pleased and asked if he could be of any help. Regis gave him a negative nod as he left the taxi to enter the station.

Regis was only gone for about five minutes, it seemed to Hilda. As he seated himself beside her he told the taxi driver to take them to Delmonico's. The taxi driver whisked around two or three blocks and they were there.

Hilda was pleased with what she saw as she approached the entrance to Delmonico's as Regis was busy with the taxi driver. Lenora had mentioned Delmonico's but had never taken her there. Lemora had said that big spenders go to Delmonico's. She wanted to see Lenora but she would have to do it another time.

As she sat waiting in the foyer of Delmonico's, she watched Regis. She wondered why she was beginning to like the man. She didn't know a lot about him and before she got more involved she wanted to know him better.

Regis smiled and offered his arm as he came walking by and then they were directed to the head waiter. The waiter pointed to another waiter who showed them to a booth. Hilda was tickled because the booths were semi-enclosed, with candles, very romantic. One side of the restaurant was a stage and a huge dance floor. Regis told her that a big band would come in later and they would be able to dance.

CHAPTER TWELVE

After getting settled, Regis said, "Mr. Tate had this all arranged, so let's have some champagne and then order. Hilda thought, "Mr. Tate had all this arranged, which sounds peculiar. How does he know all of these people? Maybe Regis does know more than he is telling me. I hope tonight maybe he will get loose enough to tell me more. I know there is something fishy about Mr. Tate and his wife but Regis doesn't want to worry me. He probably won't tell me very much because he might be afraid that I won't return."

Regis offered a toast when the waiter poured the champagne. He said, "To the most beautiful southern girl in New York and I think I am going to miss her next week."

Hilda didn't know what to say so she bent over and hugged Regis. Regis caught her around the waist and pulled her closer to him, "No one can see us, give me a little kiss." Hilda puckered and Regis gave her a lingering kiss.

The waiter approached, "Excuse me, I'll be back later." Almost in unison, laughingly, both said, "No, let's order."

After ordering, Hilda lingered with her champagne but Regis was consuming it like water and his mood was very jovial, which pleased Hilda. Deep in her mind, she thought maybe he would tell her more about the Tates.

By time the main course arrived, Regis was talking to Hilda about everything relative to the Tates, it seemed. He was in a mood she hadn't seen. He seemed different,

Regis stared at her a couple of times while she was enjoying the good food they had ordered. Hilda wondered what all this meant, but as he kept talking about the Tates, she blurted out,

"Regis, can you tell me one thing before I leave in the morning for Mississippi? Tell me how the Tates secured their wealth."

Regis' facial expression changed immediately, saying, "My southern friend giving you an answer to the question you just asked might deter you from coming back to me. The past few weeks being around you has had an effect on me to the point that I am very fond of you and am hoping that you will return after your visit home. But, if you in insist, I will go ahead and tell you about the Tates."

Looking straight at Regis, Hilda said, "Whatever the case may be, I will return because I am not taking all of my personal things on just a visit.

I am not a person just to drop everything and take another direction. My Poppa taught me to stand up for myself and other circumstances have taught me to be more responsible than most people my age. I have been through more personal things you don't know about that has caused me to make better judgments at this stage in my life."

Regis didn't say anything but motioned for the waiter. The band was late getting started, so he told the waiter to bring another magnum of champagne. The restaurant was getting packed with more people coming in. Regis reached over and held Hilda's hand.

The waiter arrived and filled their glasses, Regis cleared his throat and said, "I have told you already how I came to be with Mr. Tate. Well, it was several months before I really found out just how Mr Tate accumulated his money. It comes through a syndicate out of Boston, which he now controls, a big drug business operation, parts of the East Coast, New Orleans, Jamaica, London and Paris. Some of the people you met on your trip have dealings with him and his mob. Some are actual employees. He has been in and out of trouble with the law. While being investigated at one time, he met the woman who is now his wife. She becomes tired of the way she lives and that is why she has left him. This is not the first time that Mrs. Tate has left him but I feel this time she will not return. Now Maxine was a child that was left without parents because of a shootout with drug dealers and Mrs. Tate adopted her from the state. So far they have not had any concrete evidence that Mr. Tate is involved with drug trafficking because he has been well covered by people in high places. The less I know and say about his personal business, the better. At this stage of the game, all I look forward to is that paycheck every week. I hope this information doesn't scare you because everything is secure around the Tate compound. I am looking for you to come back because I would miss you so much."

Hilda smiled, "You have been so sweet telling me all this information and I won't be gone over a week. Probably, if you had told me this a few week ago, I would not have planned to go at this time. My Poppa wants to see me, so I am going to be with him a few days and check on Jerlene, his housekeeper."

As Regis and Hilda held hands and enjoyed their champagne, the band started playing one of Hilda's favorite songs, "That Old Black Magic." Regis pushed up from the table, pulling Hilda to her feet, they drifted out on the dance floor. They danced for the next hour it seemed to Hilda, because she didn't really want the dancing to end. She had not felt this way since Anthony Leo had held her in his arms at the high school prom. Maybe a trip home would help her decide whether she should get involved with this man or not.

Hilda opened her eyes while dancing, saying, "Regis, it is getting late and I want to be on that train to Mississippi in the morning."

Regis smiling straight into her face, kissing her fully on the lips, murmuring, "You don't have to go but if you do, a week is long enough."

Grasping her hand, Regis signed the check and they shot out the door to a taxi, taking a direct route back to the hotel.

As the taxi pulled up and they were getting out to enter the hotel lobby, Regis said smiling, "Your room or mine?" Hilda let out a chuckle and they both started laughing.

As they got off the elevator and entered the suite, they noticed a small elegant table had been set up with candles and a magnum of champagne in ice. Pulling the small card from the envelope on the table, Regis read, "Hope you are having a good time, signed Mr. Tate." He showed the card to Hilda and she said, "There must be something good about this man."

Regis said, "Since he went to all this trouble, we'll have to have one glass of champagne before we call it a day." Hilda agreed but she really didn't want to do so.

After nursing the drink for awhile, Hilda said, "Regis, I hate to rush it but it is already morning and I need some shut eye before boarding that train." She noticed that Regis was feeling no pain but yet very much in control. He stood up and kissed her three or four times and then started toward his bedroom waving as he left. Hilda was much confused as she went to bed.

Hilda was glad that they had put a wake-up call at the desk when entering the hotel because at straight up 7, the phone went off. She got her bath and into her clothes before coming out to see about Regis. She could tell he was already up and sitting as if waiting for something.

She said, "You seem all calm, cool and collected." Regis quickly replied, "I hope you want some breakfast because it will be here shortly. I am hungrier than a junk yard dog." She laughed and said, "I need a good cup of java." He shook his head saying, "If you mean coffee, it is coming."

After a moment or so, in came the waiters with a couple of tables full of breakfast foods.

They both ate like they were starved to death and having a good time. Regis finally said, "I hate to say it but we need to get you to the station. I almost wish I was going with you." Hilda said, "Well, you are welcome to come along and see how a real southern girl lives. We are a very close knit family and we'll treat you like royalty."

Staring at her as if trying to find the right words, Regis commented, "I would love to go, but under the circumstances with my employer, he would not approve me leaving right at this time. You know there's lots going on between him and his wife and anything could just blow up."

Hilda, confused, said, "Regis, do be careful because I have become very fond of you and I wouldn't want anything to happen to you."

Regis moved closed to her, hugging and kissing at the same time, saying, "I didn't know you cared for me as much as you say you do. We'll have to follow up on this when you return."

They heard a knock on the door of the suite and Regis pulled the door open and the valet had arrived for her luggage. Down the hall to the elevator they went hand in hand following the valet. As they entered the lobby, the valet directed them to the limousine.

On their way to the train station, Regis said, "Take care of yourself and let me know when you arrive. I will be at the Tate Compound waiting for your call."

Hilda squeezed his hand and said, "I will do that just for you."

Pulling into the parking area, Regis reached over hugged and kissed her several times. He then retrieved her luggage, and they walked into the lobby of the station. The attendant was announcing that the train for DC was now loading and that meant Hilda had to go the passenger platform for boarding.

At the entrance to the passenger car, Regis gave her one last hug and kiss as she boarded the train. He stood outside waiting for the train to move and as he watched through the window, he gave her a smile and waved as the train left the station. Many things went through his mind. He wondered about his infatuation with this southern girl, and thought that he might really love her. Hope of pursuing further was uppermost in his mind.

Just before arriving in DC, the train porter told Hilda that her roomette would be ready when she returned from having her evening meal in the dining car. Mr. Tate had put her in a nice little roomette so she could get some rest and as Hilda perused the site, it was very comfortable.

In DC she went to the dining room, which was just one car down, to have her evening meal. As she approached her roomette after eating, she found that her bed had been let down and was ready for the night.

Hilda was tired and she prepared herself for bed. She dozed off and didn't remember anything until the next morning somewhere in eastern Tennessee, the sun was shining in her window.

After breakfast in the dining car, she returned and the porter had fixed her roomette back into a sitting room, she began to wonder about being with her Poppa and Jerlene. It was hard to believe that she had been away almost three years. In just a few hours she would be able to see her Poppa in Meridian.

As she stared out the window of her roomette, she hoped that the visit home would be enjoyable and maybe she would be able to find some answers about her feelings for Regis but above all getting to see her baby "Gloria" one day soon.

The mid-day sun shining into her roomette window had completely relaxed her. She jumped when she heard the intercom saying, "All off at Meridian in thirty minutes." In just about five minutes the porter came to help her and he inquired if she needed any assistance in getting off. Hilda let him know quickly that she was ready to get off and her baggage was there for him to carry inside the station where her Poppa would be waiting.

The train slowed down and Hilda stayed in her roomette until it had stopped. She looked out the window and saw her Poppa on the platform staring at the train. She moved to disembark and as she did, her Poppa had his arms around her.

She was elated to see her Poppa but was not pleased at the way he looked and carried himself. He looked as if he had aged ten years. She didn't make any comments because she didn't want to hurt his feelings. From past experiences, she knew her Poppa could be easily hurt.

After getting her bag, they both settled in the pick-up truck on their way to D'Lo, After awhile, Hilda finally asked. "Poppa, how have you been doing?"

Gazing at Hilda, his expression showed that his health had not been the best in the last year. He said, "Hilda, honey, this last year has really been bad for me. It seems that I have been having sinus and colds, one right after the other. I just can't shake it. I have really been working Jerlene over time taking care of me. Also, some of her friends, who used to know her mother from Chalmette have recently been to see her. She is looking forward to seeing you and is always saying that she misses you."

Her Poppa was quiet for awhile but it seemed to Hilda he wanted to talk more. So, Hilda said, "Poppa, have you been to the doctor lately about the way you feel? Have you been doing too much lately and not resting like you always did in the afternoon? You know that I love you and want you to take care of yourself."

Mr. Webber very abruptly said, "The doctor told me I had some sinus and bronchitis and gave me some medicine but it didn't help much. Maybe by you being around for a few days it will make me feel like my old self."

As Poppa's pickup truck approached the turn off at Puckett on the way to D'Lo, Hilda thought to herself, it will be good to see the old homestead again. Flashes of incidents that she had experienced at home began to come in her mind as if she was at the movies. A great feeling came over her and she thought I will try to make the visit home, a pleasant one for her Poppa and Jerlene.

Driving up the drive-way at the home she had missed the last three years, she saw Jerlene come running out to greet them. As Hilda tried to open the door of the pickup, she almost had to push Jerlene out of the way to open it. They hugged each other just like high school teenagers, both speaking at the same time.

Jerlene said, "Miss Hilda, you must be in love, your smile just glows like this Mississippi sunshine. It is so wonderful to see you again. Maybe Mr. Webber will start feeling better, since you are here for a visit. Come on in this house and relax because I have supper almost ready and I cooked some of your favorite dishes. Remember how you loved my steak, tomato gravy and hot biscuits topped off with orange marmalade cake. Let's have a glass of red wine. Since you've been gone, Mr. Webber and I have been enjoying a glass of wine in the evening before we had supper."

After Jerlene helped Hilda get settled back in her own room, she pranced down the hallway into the kitchen. Poppa had settled down on the back porch waiting to be called for supper.

Hilda walked to the back porch and Jerlene approached with three glasses of wine. Hilda told Jerlene to sit down and have a chat while enjoying the wine before supper. Sitting there talking and sipping her wine, Hilda took notice of Poppa and knew he didn't feel too good.

After a short while, Jerlene, announced she would have supper on the table in a few minutes, so Hilda was left with her Poppa. Talking with him for awhile, she felt he was not feeling well and he was concerned about himself.

In a few minutes, Jerlene called them in for supper. As they ate, talked and asked Hilda lots of questions, it was getting dark outside. Hilda really enjoyed being home among her own surroundings. She was very glad she had decided to come home for a visit at this time because she was now worried about her Poppa's health.

After sitting awhile, Poppa said that he felt tired and that he was going to bed. Hilda told Jerlene she would help her straighten up the kitchen but Jerlene told her she knew that she was weary from the trip and needed to get some rest.

Hilda told her Poppa, "Goodnight and it was good to be home." Getting into her nightgown, she went to the kitchen to see Jerlene. Jerelene said, "Miss Hilda, Mr. Webber has not been well, as you can see. If you had not come home, I was going to call you and ask you to come see about him. Maybe he will feel better since you are here. Now, I want you to go get some rest and we'll see how things are tomorrow."

After hugging Hilda goodnight, Jerlene pranced up the hallway to her room, just like she always would do. Watching her, it gave Hilda a good feeling of being home again.

Hilda went straight to bed, hoping tomorrow would be a festive one with Poppa and Jerlene.

Upon waking, she heard noises, Jerlene was crying and as she came into Hilda's room, she heard her say, "Miss Hilda, I tried to wake up Mr. Webber so he could get ready for breakfast but I can't get him to say a word. Come on in his room and see what's the matter with him."

Hilda jumped out of bed and into Mr. Webber's room she ran. As she approached him lying in bed, she knew something was wrong. His eyes were closed as if sleeping. She put her hand on his arm trying to shake him but there was no response.

Quickly, she picked up the telephone and called Dr. Mahaffey at his home because it was Sunday morning. He informed her he would be over in just a few minutes.

When the Doctor arrived and came into the room, he immediately knew that Mr. Webber had died in his sleep during the night. He told Hilda her Daddy had been to see him a couple of days ago. He told her he would inform the funeral home on his way home.

After the Doctor left, Hilda and Jerlene went to the back porch to plan Poppa's funeral. Sitting there awhile, the funeral home van came to pick up Mr. Webber's body. Hilda told them she would be down the next day to make arrangements for his funeral. Hilda was sad but glad she was home when this happened.

Tomorrow after her visit to the funeral home, she would also make a stop by lawyer Sykes' office and ask about the will Poppa had filed with him. Poppa had informed her about the will when she left for New York almost three years ago.

She had hoped for a fun trip home but as of now things were pretty sad. Jerlene was taking Poppa's death very badly, making it worse for her to cope with the situation. Hilda said to herself, "I have got to be strong to get through this because if I show weakness, Jerlene won't be able to live here in this house as a caretaker until I return. Poppa had told me he was going to put it in the will for Jerlene to be able to do so. Tomorrow, I will be able to find out just what Poppa has done, also, I must remember to call Regis because I may be a couple of days later getting back than had planned.

Yesterday had been a bleak day at the Webber house. Today, Hilda had to go to the funeral home early and then make a trip to Lawyer Sykes' office to pick up the will Mr. Webber had given him to keep.

After Hilda and Jerlene finished the funeral planning, they

left for Lawyer Sykes in Poppa's new car he had bought only a couple of months ago. Hilda wondered why he bought the new car and now, what she was going to do with this new car. She thought, I have so much on my mind and I have to remember to call Regis when I get back to the house.

Arriving at Lawyer Sykes' office, she told Jerlene to watch the car, she would be back in a short while. As she opened the door to his office, he was sitting at his desk. He looked up and said, "Hilda, I've been expecting you. Your Dad gave me this envelope to give to you, in case something happened to him. It has been sealed for a good while, well, just about the time that you left for New York. I have no idea what is in the envelope but if you would like to open it and see what is there, now is the time, just in case you might need me to help you in any way. If you would like, go into my other office and read it. I will make a couple of calls while you look it over."

Hilda had a funny feeling as she walked to the next room and sat down on a couch. Opening the envelope, she noticed quickly her Dad's beautiful penmanship.

She began reading, but it seemed she could almost hear her Poppa's voice saying to her, "To my wonderful daughter, Hilda, whom I hope has forgiven me: All that I possess I leave to you and your daughter, Gloria Webber. I know that you are going to be criticized relative to your daughter but life is not always exactly the way you would like for it to be. Please forgive me for not being with you during these times when these occasions occur but I have asked God to forgive me for causing you this pain.

You are to be the executrix of my estate and I know that you will be able to live without seeking employment for the rest of your life, if you so desire. Your daughter is to share 50% of everything that I own. Of course, she will receive her share at the age of twenty-one, which is my wish. I do hope one day that you will be able to share some of your life with her wherever she may be. The house will be a haven for Jerlene, so let her live in it as a caretaker until death. You must see that she is duly rewarded for caring of the house until you return home, which I hope will not be too many years. But, I want you to have a good life and always remember that Poppa loved you."

Hilda could hardly keep back the tears when she went back into see Lawyer Sykes. He noticed that she had been crying and he motioned for her to sit for awhile. While sitting there, he picked up another envelope on his desk and started reading as he gave her a copy of Mr. Webber's will.

The will stated that she was the sole heir of all he possessed but he mentioned Hilda's daughter, Gloria, who would get a 50% share. Since Gloria was a child, Hilda would be the controlling heir until Gloria became of age, twenty-one. Also, the will stated that he had left a letter at the bank authorizing her complete control at his death.

After reading and discussing the will, he said, "Hilda, I didn't realize you had a daughter. Where is she now?"

Hilda braced herself, thinking of her Poppa's reputation, said, "She is with me in Boston where I am employed. She will soon be seven years of age and a beautiful child."

CHAPTER THIRTEEN

They chatted for awhile and Hilda asked Lawyer Sykes for advice. He told her that according to the will everything was in order and it would be probated before she left for Boston.

Hilda apologized to Jerlene when she returned for being away longer than anticipated. Jerlene nodded her head, saying, "Miss Hilda, I knew that it would take awhile talking to that lawyer. Let's go home and let me fix us some supper."

When they arrived home, the first thing Hilda did was call Regis. He begged Hilda to let him come at once but she finally convinced him that everything was in order and planned to arrive back on Wednesday instead of Sunday. She would be staying three days longer to do some errands after her father's funeral.

Jerlene prepared a good meal just like old times which Poppa enjoyed. While they were eating, "Jerlene said, "Let's sleep in the master bedroom where there are two beds and we can be together. Mr. Webber would want me to take care of you. I am really going to miss him, Miss Hilda."

Hilda motioned for Jerlene to come out to the back sitting room. After they had sat down, she said, "Jerlene, in Poppa's will he said you could stay on in the house as caretaker and I am to pay you for your services. Of course, I will be expecting you to take care of the property just as if it was your own. I know you will do that and if any maintenance has to be done, you can hire someone and we'll pay them. Do you want to stay on here as he suggested? I must know before I return to my position."

Hardly before Hilda could finish speaking, "Jerlene was crying, "Miss Hilda, I have no other place to go. I have no one only some distant relatives who have come to Mississippi to see me a few times. I am grateful to Mr. Webber for this privilege of having a home."

Stroking her shoulder, Hilda said, "Stop crying and remember you must stay in touch with me when I return to Boston. I hope to return back home one of these days and maybe we want be too old to enjoy a trip into Jackson like we used to do with Poppa. Now, let's go to bed because we must be strong for Poppa's funeral tomorrow afternoon.

It seemed everyone in D'Lo showed up for Mr. Webber's funeral and the Baptist Church had prepared lunch for the family. Hilda's five brothers were there with the families. Even though, they all sat together at the church, they didn't greet Hilda like brothers would greet a sister. She had not seen them in several years even though they had been living in the D'Lo community. All of her brothers knew their Dad would be leaving everything to Hilda when he died. Mr. Webber had long ago given each of them their inheritance and since that time they had not been very close to their Dad or Hilda.

Hilda, while at the funeral, heard no comments relative to having Jerlene with her. Hilda and Jerlene left the funeral in Mr. Webber's new car as several people stared as they drove off.

Arriving home, Hilda told Jerlene that she needed to rest a spell because tomorrow, Wesdnesday, she had an appointment at the bank. Jerlene told her that she needed to run an errand or two down in the quarter.

Hilda went into her old bedroom and lying there staring at the ceiling, she wondered what Regis was doing. Also, she kept thinking about what would be the reaction if he knew or anyone in D'Lo, that she had a child. She knew that sooner or later this would not be a secret anymore. Since she was nearing seven years of age, they would probably think that it was my boy friend, Leo's child. That was about the time that we were slipping around seeing each other because Poppa didn't approve of him, especially his arrogant attitude.

Another thought popped into her mind, what if the people in D'Lo knew about her Poppa's children by Jerlene who live with one of Jerlene's friends down in the quarter across the railroad track. Some must know because I have seen them with their light skin, blue eyes and blonde kinky hair. These are features, I've always wanted. Any way she said to herself, I am sleepy, let the chips fall where they may. I'll think about this another day."

She was awakened by Jerlene, saying, "Ms. Hilda, it is getting dark and you need to eat some supper. As she aroused herself, she could smell all the wonderful aroma coming down the hall from the kitchen. Jerlene was a wonderful cook.

Entering the kitchen, she could see Jerlene had everything all laid out for supper. They spent about two hours over supper talking and giggling like two teenagers. Hilda wished she could take her back to Boston. She realized that she had been missing all that southern cooking.

After supper they adjourned to the master bedroom where they reminisced about the wonderful days in the Webber household. Hilda told Jerlene before she left for Boston next Wednesday that they would discuss items relative to the house and upkeep of the yard. She mentioned to Jerlene that they would have to find a reliable person to keep the yard mowed and trimmed.

Jerlene said, "I think that I have in mind someone that you could trust to do a good job because Mr. Webber liked for his yard to be in top shape."

Hilda smiled rather faintly, thinking it could be one of the children that her Poppa had fathered with Jerlene. Not knowing for sure, Hilda thought there were at least three that could be her half sisters or brothers down in the quarter. Not wanting to question and upset Jerlene, she just didn't want to cause any disturbance at this time. As usual, she said to herself, "I will think about it tomorrow.

While Jerlene was talking, she noticed that Hilda was almost asleep, so she covered half of her body and went to bed.

Next day, Hilda told Jerlene today was the day for the bank appointment. Jerlene said, "Miss Hilda, I want you to dress-up like you are a lady from New York. Show them country hicks in that bank, just who you are." Giggling as she kept talking, "I know you are going to make their eyes pop-out. Lordy, I wish that I could be a fly on the wall and watch old lady Ross pump up her head as you walk in."

"My, my, how you do carry on," said Hilda. "Speaking of Mrs. Ross, well, between you and I, she got pregnant while in D'Lo high school and no one ever did find out who the boy was or what happened to the baby. But, she is a likeable person even though she does put on a few airs. I think that man she married has been good for her.

Hilda had to be at the bank for the 10: o'clock appointment. She stayed in her room for an hour so getting dressed before she came out sashaying around so that Jerlene could tell her if she met her approval.

Jumping up from the sofa in the main parlor, Jerlene followed Hilda on her way to the car saying,. "Miss Hilda no one in this little town has seen anyone here so beautifully dressed as you are today. You are a sight for sore eyes. When you return I will have us a light lunch waiting."

Hilda hugged Jerlene, saying, "Thanks for you help." As she pulled out of the driveway, Jerlene stood there waving.

Upon arriving at the bank, Mr. Albritton was informed and he came out to greet her. He invited her into his office. Shuffling through some papers on his desk, he looked up and said, "Miss Hilda, do you have any idea how much money your father has in this bank? Also, here is an envelope that he brought to me less than a month ago informing me to give it to you upon his death."

She looked at Mr. Albritton saying, "I don't know anything about my father's personal affairs. He never informed me about his business or banking accounts. He mentioned to me that he once owned several farms in the Delta but he sold them several years ago. I do know, if I ever needed money he was very generous. He was a great father and provider for his family. The only thing I regret is that my Mother didn't live long enough to enjoy the fruits thereof."

Mr. Albritton said, "Your father and I knew each other for years, ever since he moved here with his family from the Delta.

This I can tell you, as of now, you are a very rich young lady. Looking over the account, you are a millionaire. Do you plan to let the money stay with our bank at this time? If you do, we will have a new check book printed up changing the account before you return to Boston."

Hilda told him there would be no reason to remove the money at this time. Before leaving she opened the envelope given to her. Inside was a key and a note telling her to check the safety deposit box. She asked Mr. Albritton about the box and he showed her the room.

Opening the box, Hilda was amazed to find so much old jewelry, coins and a letter to her from Poppa. Looking at the recent date, she felt that her Poppa had a premonition he would not be living much longer. But what was so ironic was all the information about her baby Gloria's adoption giving the name of her adoptive parents including a birth certificate with appropriate information. Hilda thought how difficult it had been for her to secure some of this information when she purposely went back to the home in Natchez She asked for a large envelope so she could empty the box and Mrs. Ross was very helpful in securing it for her.

Mrs. Ross asked her what she was going to do with the house since she was told that she was going back to Boston. Hilda told her that the housekeeper would continue living there as caretaker, so she would have everything in order when vacationing back home. Mrs. Ross commented to Hilda that it was one of the most beautiful homes in the area.

Upon leaving, Hilda thanked everyone for their help and guidance. Getting into the new car to go home she wondered, why in the world did Poppa buy this new car when he loved his old truck. Now, she had to decide what to do with both because they can't just sit idle for long periods of time. If Jerlene could drive then she would let the car stay in the garage to use when she did come back for vacation. She had no idea when she would return.

Jerlene was sitting on the veranda as she drove up. After getting out of the car, she went up on the veranda to sit a spell and talk with her. Thinking about the new car, she immediately said, "Jerlene have you ever driven a car."

Jerlene jumped up and hugged Hilda profusely, saying, "Mr. Webber showed me how to drive right after you left for New York. Are you planning on letting me use the car until you get back? I have driven into Jackson several times since you been gone. If you let me, Miss Hilda, I will be careful and not show off to any of them black boys in D'Lo, honestly, I will. Why don't you let me drive us into Jackson one day before you leave and then you can see for yourself, I'm a good driver.

Hilda was at a lost for words, but she finally said, "Jerlene, that is a deal, so why not tomorrow we go into Jackson and eat lunch at the Mary Frances Tea Shop. We'll get all dressed up and you and I will prance in together, just like sisters. Poppa always said that you could pass for a white girl anywhere, so we'll prove that tomorrow."

Jerlene was beside herself as she danced around the room, singing, "I don't know what they'll do, whatever happens, I'll be with you. Yes, I am going to Jackson town to strut my stuff. Pretending that I'm a white girl will be quite enough."

Hilda couldn't believe what she was hearing as she was going down the hall to her old room. If Jerlene can drive then that would be the solution to the car.

She decided that she would call her youngest brother and see if he wanted Poppa's old truck. Calling her brothers was something that she had never done before, anyway she called Fred, the youngest of the five.

He seemed surprised when he heard her say, "Hello, Fred, this is your sister Hilda. I know that I haven't spoken to you in a long time but I was wondering if you would like to have Poppa's truck? If it stays over here idle, it will become inoperative and I thought maybe you could find some way to use it."

Fred said, "You mean to tell me that I can have Dad's truck. Dad's hasn't given me anything since he gave me my inheritance years ago. Yes, I would love to have it, just because it was his, whether it will be very useful, I don't know, but anyway, thanks. When can I pick it up?"

"Why not pick it up the first thing in the morning as I will be going into Jackson for lunch later," Hilda replied. "See you about 9: a.m," Fred quickly retorted.

Before going to bed, she told Jerlene that her brother Fred would pick up the old truck in the morning. She had solved two of her most important problems now and tonight she was looking forward to a good night's rest. Both Jerlene and Hilda were looking forward to lunch in Jackson.

Hilda woke with the sun shining through the room. The wonderful aroma of food swirling through the house brought back old memories growing up with Jerlene in the kitchen fixing breakfast for her and Poppa. Sitting on the side of her bed, she thought I must think about here and now because there wasn't time to be spent idly thinking about the past.

She called Jerlene and she was there in a flash, saying, "Miss Hilda, I was so excited about going into Jackson, I didn't get much shuteye. Your brother has been sitting on the back porch for quite a spell because he told me not to wake you."

"Please hand me my robe and tell him I be out in a few minutes," Hilda quickly stated. In a way, she was glad that she was going to see her brother again. She saw him at the funeral for the first time in two or three years. She used to wonder why the family wasn't closer but after Poppa gave the five boys their inheritance as they had requested, occasionally she would see them.

Slinging on her robe, she walked to the back porch. Her brother was outside looking over the old truck. Hilda said, "Think you can use it, if you can, it's yours. Poppa was crazy about that old truck and I really wonder why he bought the new car."

Fred commented, "You know our Dad at one time had lots of money and the one reason why us boys got together and approached Dad to give us our inheritance was because we didn't expect him to have it later on when he died. I don't know anything about the will he filed but I am sure that he left you with enough money to enjoy life."

Hilda felt like he was fishing for information, so to ease his mind, she said, "Poppa always looked after my interest. If I wanted to, I could come home and live comfortably but I want to do something worthwhile with my life. I have a great position with some good people that respect me. I love D'Lo but I want to get out and see other places in this beautiful world before I hang up my hat back home."

Fred looked stunned to Hilda as he was given the keys to the truck. He smiled and waved to both Hilda and Jerlene as he drove out of the driveway.

Hilda shouted, "Jerlene get out those clothes and let's get ready for the big city. Purposely, I didn't eat much breakfast because I wanted a good lunch at the Mary Frances." Slapping Jerlene on her fanny as she went up the porch steps, saying, "I hope you don't hurt us driving that car to Jackson. I am looking forward to a great day."

When they walked out of the house to get in the car they looked like two sisters hugging and carrying on about how good each looked. Hilda noticed the way Jerlene carried herself and got in the car as if she knew just what to do. She maneuvered the car so well that Hilda felt she had been driving it quite a bit. Going up highway 49 toward Jackson, she felt safe with Jerelene at the wheel.

There was not much conversation on the way into Jackson. Jerlene knew where the Mary Frances was located and she got into a parking place nearby just like a pro. This caused Hilda to think, well, I want have to worry about the car when I leave.

After parking nearby, they walked across the street to the entrance of the restaurant. As they entered, they both looked at each other, smiled and winked. A waitress came forward and showed them to a table.

As they seated themselves, Hilda said, "Jerlene, I want you to order whatever you like because that is what I am going to do. I am so hungry, I could eat a horse."

Jerlene said, "Now watch you manners because I see a good looking guy staring at us."

Hilda quickly said, "Jerlene, he is giving you the eye, not me." Both of them looked at him and started giggling.

"Last time I was here with Poppa, there was a bunch of legislators, mostly old men, but the scene has changed as you can see," said Hilda.

As Hilda looked up, the man that was looking at them and smiling had approached their table. He said, "Pardon me for intruding but do you all come here often? I knew that Jackson had a bunch of beautiful women but this is the first time to see you two. I am a new state senator from north Mississippi and if you would like, I would be most happy to give you a tour of the capitol."

Hilda flipped back quickly, "We're just here for lunch and a little shopping on Capitol Street. We live in the country, in the big city of D'Lo." By now both of them were giggling like two young girls.

Jerlene thought, I wonder what would happen if that man knew that I was a black girl. She blinked her beautiful eyes at him, still giggling.

He looked sort of stunned, saying, "Here is my card, whenever you plan to come back into Jackson, let me know because I would like to invite you both to dine with me." Some other men were leaving and he joined them, saying, "Goodby."

It was getting close to 2: p.m. as they left the restaurant. Driving home was a talkative affair it seems, Jerlene was bubbling over and Hilda was a good listener. Hilda felt less worried about Jerlene taking care of the house and the car since their soiree today. Actually, she felt that Jerlene was a better driver than her.

Arriving home, Jerlene parked the car in the garage while Hilda waited on the front porch. Hilda thought, today was just a beautiful day. Jerlene joined her on the porch. They sat there for an hour talking about Hilda going back to Boston in two or three days. Jerlene was letting her know that it was going to be lonesome without Poppa and as she mentioned him, Hilda could see tears in her eyes.

The sun was beginning to set and shadows had encompassed the whole house. Hilda said, "I must get me a good night's sleep so I can start packing my bag tomorrow. Jerlene, I want you to help me get my clothes together. Also, we will need to go to the bank and fix you with an account, so you can pay the small bills that might occur relative to the house. I am going to pay you $200.00 a month for your work around here if that is satisfactory with you."

Jerlene said, "Why so much, you are giving me a home? Your family has kept me all these years in everything I need. You know that I will take care of everything, or die trying."

"I want you to have some spending money, in case you want something," stated Hilda. "You know I am depending on you to take care of the place as if you own it and if you can't, you can contact me immediately. Keep in contact with me at least every other week."

Jerlene said, "Miss Hilda, you know I will do exactly as you request regarding everything. But, I have a surprise for you before you go back to Boston. It seems that you have forgotten that the day before you leave is your birthday. I remember when you were born even though I was only 10 or 11. I am planning a small party for us to celebrate your 28th birthday. Three or four of my friends from the quarter will be here to help me. These friends will be helping me while you are away so I thought it would be nice for you to meet them before you leave. You may have already met one of the boys, Cicero and my good friend Katie Mae."

With a stunned gaze, Hilda said, "Well, how do you do, if I am 28 then you must be about 39. I do appreciate you thinking of me and tell your friends they will be welcome here at Webber house."

Hilda's mind was really grinding and thoughts were bumping into each other. Would she see the rest of Poppa's children by Jerlene? Cicero looked very much like Poppa and I will be able to tell if anyone else favors my Poppa. She was really looking forward to her birthday party now.

Hilda said, "Jerlene, I am looking forward to your party for me on Tuesday but we had better get some sleep as I need to go to the bank first thing in the morning."

Jerlene excused herself and said, "I am going to clean up the kitchen and I will go to bed in a short while."

There was a lull over the whole house it seems as Jerlene left to do her chores before bedtime. Hilda drifted away after going to bed.

Both slept late the next morning but Jerlene had gotten up earlier than Hilda to prepare breakfast. Hilda decided that she would get ready to go to the bank before eating. They lingered over breakfast talking for about two hours.

Jerlene looking sad said, "Miss Hilda, I am going to miss your company when you leave. At night this house will be like a ghost castle with me here by myself."

"You know that you can have your friends, the ones you have invited to my birthday party to visit you. All you need to do is take care of everything here as I requested. Act with proper judgment about what you do," Hilda retorted.

Jerlene smiled saying, "Miss Hilda, I completely understand everything you are saying. I am not going to cause you any trouble, I would die first. I owe that to your father, Mr. Webber."

After returning from the bank, Hilda called Jerlene from the back porch requesting her to sit down with her and she would explain about the bank account.

CHAPTER FOURTEEN

She said, "Jerlene, this is your signature card which I want you to sign so I can drop off at the bank. It gives you permission to write checks to pay bills relative to the house. This is your check book and each check is numbered, so you can keep up with them as they are written. Every month you can write yourself a check for $200.00 for spending money you can use as you wish. I have put $5000.00 in the bank account and I will replenish it when needed but that I will take care of myself. Do you understand everything that I have gone over?

"Yes, Miss Hilda, I understand and remember doing this one time for Mr. Webber when he felt bad and wanted me to write something for him. You are as generous as your Poppa. Thank you so much, Miss Hilda, I want let you down."

As they both retired to bed, Hilda thought about tomorrow. She had one more day before leaving for Boston. Jerlene was going to take her to catch the train in Meridian. After all she had to trust Jerlene with the car so this would be a test as to her responsibility. Actually, she felt good about leaving everything in Jerlene's care.

Next day was packing day for Hilda. She had Jerlene running around the bedroom helping her decide just what she should take with her. She told Jerlene to get all of her clothes out of the closet and if she could wear them, then she could have them. Hilda laughed as Jerlene tried on dress after dress until she was given out.

Both of them sat on the floor and Hilda starting planning with Jerlene about the trip to Meridian on Wednesday. Jerlene said, Miss Hilda, I am sure everything will be alright and I will be careful coming back by myself. I love to drive that new car."

Hilda quickly said, "Jerlene, I know you can handle everything as we planned. When you get back, write me a letter, because I will be expecting to hear from you. Also, I want you to call the phone company and make sure it is working again, Poppa had told me that it wasn't working properly. I want us to contact each other at least a couple of times a month and more if needed."

"Miss Hilda, I will be happy to do as you say," Jerlene said with a big smile.

Hilda got up from the floor and said, "We'd better get to bed, it's getting later than I thought."

There had been a thunderstorm during the night and it was still raining when Hilda and Jerlene sat on the back porch having breakfast. The aroma of coffee, bacon and fresh bread filled Hilda's nostrils as she thought, my, my, I am going to miss this when I get back to Boston.

Hilda told Jerlene that she would have to be in Meridian the next day by 3: p.m. to catch the train so they could leave early enough to have lunch at Weidman's. That was the restaurant everyone was talking about which was owned by an old Meridian family.

Late in the afternoon, Hilda asked Jerlene to take her for a drive around D'Lo, Mendenhall and Magee. As they drove through each town several people were on the streets Hilda knew and she waved at them. The people wondered who was chauffering Miss Hilda Webber these days. Hilda wanted to see if there had been any majestic changes around any where. She came to the conclusion that it seemed that everything was on a standstill.

Upon returning to the house, Jerlene had a real surprise for Hilda. As she drove up to the house, Hilda noticed three or four people sitting on the front porch. As Jerlene parked the car, she started singing, "Happy Birthday, Miss Hilda" and the others on the porch chimed in.

Hilda was completely stunned because she had forgotten about the birthday party Jerlene had planned for her. Hilda saw Katie Mae, Jerlene's friend for years who lived across the tracks in D'Lo. She hugged her and looked around at the other three children who were just about adults. Immediately, Hilda could see her Poppa's favor in all three including Cicero, whom she had met before she left for New York. She thought, these are my half sisters and brother. Just think if they knew how much money my Poppa had left me, what would they do? Would they try to claim some of it, after all Jerlene has never openly told her that Poppa was the father of these children. Jerlene always said that they were Katie Mae's family. But it was so obvious to Hilda they favored her Poppa so much. More so since she saw them together today. One of the girls had beautiful blonde, kinky hair with blue eyes. All were light skin with Mr. Webber's facial features. When Jerlene would go away on vacation, her Poppa always told her that she had gone to visit friends in New Orleans but one time Hilda had seen her in the Quarter. All these thoughts going through her mind made her dizzy.

After getting her composure, Hilda said, "This is a great surprise, and I am so happy that you all came to help Jerlene wish me a happy birthday before I leave tomorrow for Boston. I hope you all will help Jerlene when she needs you while I am away as she will be staying here as my caretaker. All of you mean a lot to both of us."

Katie Mae had cooked a huge cake and brought it for the occasion. Everyone had cake and talked until dark. The sun was going down over D'Lo rocks when the party broke up. Hilda hugged everyone as they left.

Later thinking over the day's activities, Hilda was full of questions but didn't dare question Jerlene about the three children that were with Katie Mae. She thought, why bother, it's all in the past and better to have peaceful relationships and trust in life at this time.

Wednesday was a full day for Hilda. Arising early and getting on the highway toward Meridian was easily to accomplish as they drove out of the driveway on their trip to the train station. Hilda felt very good about Jerlene as she drove like she had been doing it day in and day out.

Arriving in Meridian around 12:30 pm, they stopped at Weidman's for lunch. Both of them enjoyed being together for the hour before boarding the train. Hilda asked her if there was anything she needed to discuss before getting on the train.

Jerlene said, "Miss Hilda, I feel like I can handle what you have asked me to do. Don't worry none about anything. If something comes up I can't handle, I will contact you."

Hilda felt good about leaving the house in Jerlene's hands as she waved to her from the steps of the train. Turning to go further into the coach, the train started to move and as the porter assisted her to her roomette, she saw Jerlene still waving on the station platform.

The past few days passed so fast, it seemed to Hilda, as she sat in her roomette. Her Poppa was gone and coming back to the house in D'Lo will never be the same again. She almost broke down and cried but she felt it would be much more difficult for her if she let go. She knew that it would happen sooner or later, maybe when she saw Regis at the station in New York. By this time tomorrow afternoon she would be there.

The porter came along to see if she wanted anything and she asked him to prepare her bed as she wanted to retire early. She went to the dining room and ate supper, then read awhile before retiring.

The night went fast and when Hilda woke up on Thursday morning, the train was on its way to New York. Hilda could tell that it seemed to be cooler and she dressed for the early fall weather. Also, she wanted to look good for Regis and anticipated seeing him around 3: p.m.

She had lunch and then retired to her roomette. While waiting for the remainder of the trip into New York, many things went through her mind. First, and foremost, she didn't want to let anyone know, especially Regis, that her Poppa had left her plenty of money. She wanted to keep her position and everything at the Tate compound just as it was when she left. The situation with her daughter, Gloria, she would settle with her later when she got older. One day, she felt that the secret of her having a daughter would be exposed. Saying to herself, "I will worry about that when the time comes. Whatever happens, I will be able to deal with it, because my Poppa left me prepared for the situation."

The porter startled her as he knocked on the door of her roomette, saying, "The train is due in Grand Central Station in twenty minutes."

The porter picked up her baggage and moved toward the door of the car. Coming into the station, Hilda peaked out the big window and she saw Regis standing on the platform. She thought as she gazed at him, he really is a handsome man.

The train stopped and Hilda moved to the door of the car. As she was going down the steps, Regis reached out with a big hug. They seemed glad to see each other, both talking at the same time. Hilda was emotionally overcome as she kept hugging and crying in Regis's arms.

Regis said, "My, my, I've missed you so much. You seem to have been gone a month. I know you have been through a lot in the few days you have been gone. Let's get in the limo and head for home."

As they walked to the limo that Regis had parked nearby, Hilda said, "Regis, I am so glad that you came to meet me. If I keep crying, it's because I have not had a shoulder that I could cry on or anyone that I could talk with. Thanks so much for being here."

They didn't stop to eat supper on the way back to Boston. Regis said that he had been asked by Mr. Tate to run some errands, no matter how late it was when they arrived.

They arrived at the Tate compound about 6:30 pm and as they pulled up in the parking area, Mr. Tate came running out, saying, "Regis, I need you just as soon as you can put Hilda's luggage in her room."

Mr. Tate said, "Hilda, you and I will have a talk tomorrow, get settled in, everything is fine here and we're glad that you are back and sorry to hear about the death of your father. Maxine, I know will be glad to see you."

Regis carried her luggage to her room and as he left he said, "I'll see later when I return and so glad that you are back with us."

Maxine ran into Hilda's room crying and mumbling, "Miss Hilda, I am so glad to see you. I've missed you so much. Tomorrow I want you to tell me what you have been doing. I have not been anywhere since you left. I love you so much."

Hilda calmed Maxine down by holding her hands and telling her that she had missed her very much. While sitting there talking, Maxine fell asleep against her. This made Hilda think that the poor child had not been sleeping very well. She covered her with a small coverlet from her bed. Hilda sat for awhile looking at Maxine wondering what her Gloria was doing this time of day.

Hilda moving from Maxine's side didn't disturb her one iota, because she was sound asleep by now.

Hilda's door came open and in walked Mrs. Styne wanting to know if she could assist in any way before the evening meal. Mrs. Styne said, "Maxine had trouble sleeping and the first couple of days she wouldn't let me leave the room at night. So glad that you are back and sorry to hear about your father. I'll be downstairs if you need me."

Looking at the clock in her room, she noticed it was just about time that dinner would be served, so she decided downstairs she would go. As she walked into the dining room, she saw Regis sitting at their ususal table. Smiling as she walked in, he said, "It's about time you showed up, I've been waiting for a few minutes hoping you would."

Hilda was shocked, looking around the dining room, saying, "Who are all these people? I've never seen some or at least noticed them before."

Regis commented, "Mr. Tate had a board meeting and a party for some of his employees last week-end and some are still here conferring with him. I suppose most will clear out before the day or by tomorrow. After we get through eating, let's you and I take a drive. I need to talk with you about something that happened while you were gone."

Hilda looked confused saying, "I am with you but let's not eat so fast. I am trying to unwind from these past few days. You know

I am so glad to be back so I can talk with someone because I am going to miss my Poppa."

Lingering over dinner and talking for awhile over a glass of wine, Hilda finally said, "Regis, if you are ready let's go for that ride. I need some fresh, New England air.

Leaving the dining area, Hilda saw Mrs. Styne, asking her to check on Maxine that she would be back in a short while. Mrs. Styne smiled approvingly as they left her.

Regis had the limo parked in the driveway because he had a ride planned with Hilda before going to bed. He wanted to get her caught up on all the events that occurred while she was gone. So he decided to go to the Boston Commons for a walk. It might be a bit chilly but nice for walking.

Driving along, he said, "Let's park at the Boston Commons and take a walk." Hilda said, "That's a good idea, I need a little exercise before I go to bed. Anyway, I am curious about what you wanted to tell me."

Quickly, Regis said, "Really, lots of things happened which you don't need to worry you pretty, little head about. But, the one thing that happened that was tragic, you remember the Langley's from Hartford?

All the color went out of Hilda's face hearing the name Langley, as she listened intently. She said, "What's wrong?"

Regis looking dazed, saying, "Both Mr. and Mrs. Jason Langley were killed instantly in a freaky auto accident and their daughter, Gloria was hospitalized but is doing nicely as of now. She will be brought from the hospital to live here at the Tate compound for awhile, so I was told by Mr. Tate two or three days ago. One of Mr. Langley's distant relatives has asked the courts' permission to take the child to Greenville, Mississippi to live with her. But, in a will written up when they adopted Gloria from some home in Mississippi, that he stipulated that she would be in the care of the Tate family if anything happened to them. The relative from Mississippi according to Mr. Tate was only interested in what inheritance the Langleys had left. So you see, you might be having another child to look after. If you do, then you should ask Mr. Tate for more money or at least I would. He has already hired a registered nurse to be on duty when the child is moved here."

By this time, Hilda's head was in a spin. She had to keep calm and not show too much emotion. But, she said, "Regis is the child going to be ok? Tell me how she is doing or do you know? After all, she is just a child with no mother or father. Poor child, I will be glad when we can see her."

Regis said, "She maybe here before the week-end. She is going to be alright. With a little physical therapy, she will learn to walk again, so the doctors tell Mr. Tate."

In Hilda's world, everything had suddenly changed, her mind was doing loops, wondering what her next strategy would be relative to Gloria. She needed to get back to her room so she could try to think straight in what avenues she would have to take or decisions make. She may have to compromise her own reputation to try to help her daughter Gloria. She might even have to acquire an attorney if need be.

Suddenly she said, "Regis, let's get back so I can check on Maxine. The child hasn't slept very well since I left because she fell asleep holding on to me when I returned today. Mrs. Styne is now with her until I get back. Also, keep me posted regarding the Langley child. Mr. Tate maybe wanting to talk with me as he stipulated when I arrived. I hope you don't get too far away until I get situated back on the job. You know I like to know you're nearby."

Regis was all smiles as they drove back to the compound. As they parted, he hugged and kissed her, saying, "You know my phone number, anytime you need me, just call."

Walking into her room, Hilda threw herself on the bed and started crying. She didn't want to wake Maxine so she went into the bathroom and just exploded it seems. She didn't see Mrs. Styne when she opened the bathroom door asking what was wrong.

Mrs. Styne said, Miss Hilda what is the matter? Are you ill, can I do somethng?

Mumbling but coherent, Hilda said, "Mrs. Styne, nothing is wrong, I was just thinking of the poor, little Langley child losing her parents. Of course, she was an adopted child but she had been with them almost ten years. I am sure that she had learned to love them as they were so good to her."

"By the way, Mr. Tate said he wanted to talk with you, when you and Regis returned," uttered Mrs. Styne.

Immediately, Hilda got up and started downstairs to see if Mr. Tate was in his office. When she approached his office, she noticed he was just staring into space.

She said, "Hello," and he looked up at her saying, "Hilda, it looks like your job will be having more responsibility than you might have anticipated. You remember the Langleys, our friends from Hartford. They were killed in a tragic auto accident two days after you left for Mississippi. Their daughter, Gloria, was injured but is doing nicely and will be coming here to live in a day or two. I was in total shock for a couple of days when I was notified. Years ago when they adopted her, they stipulated in their will that she was to be in my custody if anything happened to them, so that is the reason for her coming here. I know it will be more work for you but your salary will be increased because you are so good with children. Also, a nurse will be here on duty day and night.

By the way, Mrs. Tate and I have been amicably divorced. She has moved to the Bahamas with her mother and seems to be very happy. I am sorry about the loss of your father but time will heal everything. Thanks again for your good service to my organization, You know we look upon you and Regis as family."

Upon leaving she said, Mr. Tate, "I treasure your friendship. Now, you don't really have to raise my salary but that is left up to you. I will do everything to make your load easier to carry. I will be back in my old routine in a couple of days."

When she got back to her room, the phone was ringing. As she picked up the receiver, Regis said, "You and Mr. Tate must have had a long conversation. This is the third time I have tried to get you. I know it is late so I will see you at breakfast, love you."

Hilda tossed and turned all night long. When she got up to dress for breakfast, she felt like she had been up all night. She vowed to get a nap in the afternoon so that when Gloria came she would be feeling better.

Upon entering the dining room, she wondered where Regis was, as he was usually at their regular table. It wasn't long before he came in, saying, "I hope you have a nice day because the Langley girl will be here in the afternoon, so I was just informed by Mr. Tate.

Hilda said, "Relax and tell me all about it because I was given that clue by Mr. Tate last evening when we had our chat. She will have one of the bedrooms next to Maxine. I do hope they get along together. They should because Gloria is only a year older. Anyway, with Mrs. Styne staying and a nurse coming on full time means that you and I will have some time together."

Smiling brightly, Regis said, "I think I am going to like that. Let's finish our breakfast and go for an early morning ride down the boulevard to the park. It is such a beautiful morning but the weather is getting chilly this time of the year."

So many things were turning over in Hilda's brain, like what if they knew that Gloria was really my daughter, would it be difficult for her to legally be proclaimed as her real mother. She knew that she had a birth certificate but would the courts recognize it, if she tried to say that she was her daughter.

Regis reached over and touched her shoulder, because her mind was way out and seemingly she couldn't hear what he was saying, but she managed to say, "I am sorry, but my mind was playing tricks on me thinking about Gloria Langley. Yes, I think an early morning ride would clear my head."

The morning sunshine covered the whole world, it seemed to Hilda. The crispy weather was moving into the area and she thought to herself, this isn't the weather that she really liked. As they rode along Regis held her hand and it made her feel more secure. Every now and then she would look over at Regis and give him a smile. There was very little conversation but a lot of body language between the two before they returned to the compound.

Pulling into the compound parking area, Regis said, "I have a few errands to do but will see you at lunch. Thanks for your time because I loved every minute."

As Hilda proceeded to the second floor to check on Maxine, her mind was really thinking about Gloria who was expected to arrive sometime in the afternoon. The elation of being able to see her daughter every day seemed to just sweep her away. She was anxious to find out if the accident had left any permanent damages to her body. So many things were going through her mind so she decided that she would lie down for awhile as Mrs. Styne was involved with Maxine at the moment.

The telephone rung in Hilda's room and groggily she answered it, saying, "I'm sorry but would you speak up."

Regis said, "Hilda, this is Regis, I'm sorry if I woke you. Are you coming to lunch with me? I'm downstairs waiting at our table. Mr. Tate just told me that Gloria Langley would be arriving in about two hours."

Answering quickly, she said, "Just give me a few minutes until I get myself together and dress. I had a nap and woke up hungry. We certainly want to give Gloria a good reception when she arrives. I know the child misses her parents."

Regis was at the usual table when Hilda arrived an half hour later. He was all smiles from ear to ear. While he had been waiting for her, his mind was telling him that he was falling in love with her. Regis had never been in love before but he had been with many women in his day. When he arrived in America, he found out women were different emotionally, more secure than in Europe, where it seemed that a fling was just a fling. Of course, his main objective for coming to America was to go into the theatre and it was still in the back of his mind when he could financially do so. Maybe when he saved up enough money, he could spend some time with auditions in New York.

Hilda said, "What's the matter, you act like you are somewhere else."

Regis grinned at her, saying, "I was sitting here thinking about you and me. Also, I am sorry that I woke you. I bet you were sleeping good. When you answered, you seemed so far away. But, I knew that you needed to eat and get yourself together before Gloria's arrival."

"I am glad that you called me," exclaimed Hilda. She stared into his eyes while eating, wondering if she would be happy in a commitment to this man. He was different from her first love but some how she had a deep feeling for him. What would he think if he knew that I was Gloria's real mother or that her Poppa had left her very wealthy? Who knows I might have to tell him one of these days.

Regis commented that he had to run some errands for Mr. Tate and would see her later. Hilda got up to leave and as she went out of the dining area, Mr. Tate came out of his office. He said, "Hilda, Gloria will be here very shortly and I would like for you to be here with me when she arrives."

Hilda said, "Mr. Tate, I will be back shortly for Gloria's arrival." As she proceeded up the stairs a dizzy feeling of excitement enveloped her as she thought about being able to see her baby girl. Many thoughts went through her mind, would they have a good rapport, is she spoiled, would she get along with Maxine. But as usual, to herself, she said, "I'll worry about that tomorrow."

Going into her living area, she sat down for a moment with all kind of thoughts going through her head. She said to herself, "I could really blow this whole episode apart just by telling Mr. Tate that Gloria was her real daughter. I will just have to play it cool and see what the future has in store for me and Gloria."

She heard noises outside and she immediately left to meet with Mr. Tate. As she approached the foyer of the Tate complex, she saw a woman with a beautiful young girl which looked older than her ten years. Mr. Tate came up to this lady and turning around said to Hilda, "Miss Hilda this is Gloria and her nurse, Miss Kim, who is from the state Child Welfare Department.

Hilda felt like she was going to lose control of herself and she didn't want to show any outward emotion. She immediately stooped down and said, "Hello, Gloria."

Gloria said, "Hello, how are you today? I am a little tired from riding but I will feel better tomorrow."

Hilda noticed that she even acted older than her age and such a beautiful child, probably from being around older people. It was obvious that she did favor her Poppa.

Mr. Tate asked Hilda and Miss Kim to come into his office for a chat. They did so, leaving Gloria sitting in the foyer where they could see her.

Mr. Tate thanked Miss Kim for accompanying Gloria to his household. Miss Kim explained to them that Gloria had recuperated nicely from the accident. Also, she mentioned that a couple of the Langley relatives had been to see her and wanted to take her back to their home in Mississippi. Of course, that was impossible since Gloria had been legally left in Mr. Tate's guardianship. Also, from what she heard them say, they were going to try to break that ruling by filing a suit since they were relatives of the Langleys. She brought all of Gloria's clothes which were in the suitcases sitting in the foyer. She didn't want to bring any toys of which she had many. She tries to act older than she really is.

While Hilda sat there listening, her mind became so confused because she felt that one day she would be trying to prove that she was Gloria's biological mother.

CHAPTER FIFTEEN

Mr. Tate broke up the chit chat by saying, "Miss Kim, thanks for bringing Gloria to me. Gloria really looks fine after what she has experienced. Miss Hilda will take over from here until the nurse arrives tomorrow."

Upon leaving, Miss Kim, told Mr. Tate that everything was in order since he had assumed responsibility for Gloria's welfare.

Hilda started to leave with Gloria in hand but Mr. Tate called her into his office.

Mr. Tate said, "I am leaving Gloria in your hands, the same as with Maxine. When the nurse arrives tomorrow, she will be on duty at all times and at your command. You will be in charge of her and also, Mrs. Styne as she has agreed to stay as long as you need her. If you need me in any way, please feel free to contact me whether I am on the complex or not. My business is very good at this time and I may be away for periods of time, but Regis will always know how to get in touch with me. He, too, will be of help to you whenever you need him. Thanks so much for being here."

As she left Mr. Tate, she was overwhelmed with his kindness. She felt at the moment that if she confided in him about Gloria being her biological daughter, that he might just understand. But, that would be risky at this time, so as usual she confided to herself, I'll worry about that tomorrow.

Arriving in the upstairs living quarters, she heard Gloria talking to someone. As she entered the room Mrs. Styne had assigned as Gloria's room, Maxine said, "Miss Hilda, Gloria and I have been talking about you. Gloria told me that you were not only beautiful but seemed to be a nice lady."

Gloria quickly said, "I surely said that. Also, I told her that I didn't like to play with toys very much anymore."

Hilda said, "Well, let's sit down here and talk for awhile. I need to tell you that your nurse, Miss Booth, will be here tomorrow. She will arrange a schedule for you so that you will know what kind of routine you will be involved in each day. Part of the day will be involved with school and then there will be play time. I will be around at all times to see and check on you every day. We'll have a great time together."

Mrs. Styne had unpacked all of Gloria's dresses and hung them in her room and neatly put other items in the chests. Hilda thought, I surely would miss her if she wasn't here.

Looking around to see if everything was in order, she said, "Girls, I think we should get you ready for bedtime."

Walking toward the entrance to her room, Gloria said, "I don't need any help to get ready for bed so I will say, goodnight to everyone."

Hilda was so surprised to hear this from an eleven year old but then she thought, maybe this is what she has been accustomed to doing.

Hilda waited awhile before going into Gloria's room so she proceeded to look in on Maxine. When she entered Maxine's room, she was already in bed. Maxine raised her arms and Hilda bent down for a hug, saying, "Goodnight."

When Hilda got around to Gloria's room, she was sitting on the bed reading a little book. Hilda sat down beside her and she kept reading. Hilda bragged on how well she read and it seemed to please Gloria.

Gloria said, "My mother and father had plans for me to go to a private school in Switzerland when I became twelve years old. I hope that I get to do so because they talked to me about it not long before the accident. Mr. Tate knows about the plans they had for me. I want to get back into my music. Miss Hilda is there a piano in this house?

Hilda said, "I haven't seen one but there might be one but if not we'll see that you have a piano even if I have to purchase one for you. So, you can go ahead and get into bed. She hugged her and whispered, "Goodnight, think about what kind of piano you would like."

Back in her room, lying in bed, it was difficult for her to believe that Gloria acted so mature for her age. She was afraid that being with Maxine would be boring. She was also anxious to hear Gloria play the piano. The first thing on tomorrow's agenda would be to see if there was a piano on the compound and if not there would be one before dark. She would lasso Regis for this project.

Next morning, the day started off with the arrival of Miss Booth and she took over just as if she had been there before. She had both Gloria and Maxine under her control before the morning became afternoon. Hilda was very pleased with her aura and had no intention of telling her what to do because she had everything under control.

At breakfast, Hilda sat with Regis and watched Miss Booth as she talked and laughed with both Maxine and Gloria. It made her feel good because both acted like they approved of her already. Hilda commented to Regis, "Why bother when everything is going great."

Regis laughed saying, "You know this means you and I will have more time together."

"Don't get too excited you know I still have my job to do," snapped Hilda.

Regis said, "I am going downtown shortly. How about going along with me?"

Hilda thought of the piano, so she said, "Is there a piano anywhere on this complex? Gloria wants a piano so she can practice her music.

Regis quickly said, "No, I haven't seen one anywhere and I have been all over the compound."

Hilda waving her hands saying, "Hold on for a short while and I will accompany you downtown because I will be purchasing a piano for Gloria this day. Maybe we can get it moved here today because she wants a piano as soon as possible. I haven't heard her play but I was told that she is very talented. I am really excited to hear her perform."

As Regis left the dining area, he said, "You know my number, when you get ready to go, just call me. Smiling, he said, Mr. Tate told me to be at your beck and call, so here I am.

Hilda was calling Regis within thirty minutes saying she would be downstairs right away. Grabbing her purse and making sure that her check book was inside, she was on her way. Her thoughts were to have a piano within the Tate compound before dark.

As she approached Regis, he said with a grin from ear to ear, "Are you ready and if so, get in beside me."

Hilda gave him a slap on the arm as she slid in trying to get as close as possible just to annoy him. But, it seems that it had a reverse effect. He looked too satisfied.

Driving out of the compound, Hilda slid her hand across the back of his neck. Instantly, he said, "Now that is something different and you don't want to make me wreck this limo. I get emotionally involved when you rub my neck."

Immediately, she put both hands in her lap. saying, "Let's get serious. Do you know of a place that sells pianos and if so, take me there?"

"Yes, and since you asked earlier, been trying to figure out which place I should start first. I think the one I have in mind will be the best one. That place is called the Music Circle which is nearby."

No more than ten minutes they were parking before a huge store with pianos gazing out huge windows.

After getting out of the limo, Hilda stood outside looking at the pianos from the street. Regis caught her by the hand saying, "Come on let's go inside."

As they walked inside, a salesman approached them. Hilda said right off, "If I buy a piano right now will it be delivered today?"

The man seemed to be bewildered and stuttered saying, "I suppose that would be possible but first I must ask my supervisor. Can you give me the delivery address?

She gave him the address, saying, I will be looking around while you are gone. Also, I would like for someone to give me a demonstration of the piano that I might like."

Smiling, he said, "I would be glad to play something for you. Just give me a few moments."

In his absence, Hilda and Regis looked at several pianos. Regis could tell that one piano caught Hilda's eye but he didn't say a word. He wanted her to make the decision. It was a beautiful small grand, black, lacquered piano.

The salesman returned saying that the piano could be delivered before dark. Immediately, Hilda told him that she would like for him to play something on the small grand. He played several songs and she was pleased with the sound.

In her mind, she was convinced that this was the piano for Gloria, so she asked, "What is the price?

He blurted out, "Seventy five hundred dollars but I have permission to let it go for five thousand."

Immediately, she said, "I want it and want it delivered today. Can I give you a check ?

The salesman's eyes lit up saying, "Of course, but will need some identification. It will be delivered this afternoon late."

Hilda showed him her bank identification plus driver's license. In so doing, Regis just stood there in awe, watching her write out a check for five thousand dollars and handing it to the salesman. His mind was working on all forty cylinders, saying to himself how can someone with her position have that much money to spend on a complete stranger.

She noticed Regis as she was writing the check and when she looked up and saw him staring at her, she just smiled. She knew there would be questions later but as usual she said to herself, "I'll worry about that tomorrow."

As they were going to the limo, Regis said, "I have a couple of errands to do before we leave for the compound."

Hilda shook her head smiling as she got into the limo. Immediately, upon getting relaxed, she said, "I will have to decide where to position the piano when it arrives later. I think that the small room near their playroom would be ideal because she could close the door when practicing."

Regis shook his head in approval even though his boggled mind was still on edge relative to Hilda spending that much money as if she was a rich lady. After doing his errand, on the way home, he refused to ask any questions.

Arriving back at the compound, Hilda went immediately to look at the small room she mentioned to Regis. On the way to the room, she ran into Mr. Tate and she told him about buying the piano for Gloria. At first, he acted like he was in total shock, especially after Hilda told him how much it cost. She explained to him that Gloria was always mentioning that she wanted to get back to her music studies. In leaving he told her that she made a good decision and that she would be reimbursed for the money. Hilda felt rather perturbed but she caught herself before she said too much which might be suspicious. Thinking as usual, saying to herself, "I'll worry about that tomorrow."

Hilda retired to bed saying not a word about a piano to Gloria. She tossed a bit thinking about what Mr. Tate and even Regis would probably say the next day about her purchase, but she finally got to sleep.

Going down to breakfast the next morning, she saw that the piano had been moved. When she sat down at the usual table with Regis, he said, "I know you noticed the piano has been moved. Well, Mr. Tate had it moved to the little room upstairs where you wanted it. I know Gloria is going to be elated when she sees her new piano."

Smiling at Regis, she said, "Sometimes you do the sweetest things. I know you had that piano moved because I mentioned where I would like it to be. I know it must have been a job to get it up those stairs."

Putting his hand over on hers, Regis said, "No, five of the maintenance men moved it about ten o'clock last evening. It is just the place for the piano which can be private for Gloria to do her practicing. Also, by the way, Mr. Tate wants to talk with you when you finish breakfast. He will be in his office all morning."

"Thanks for everything and will see you later," chimed Hilda as she left going to Mr. Tate's office.

As Hilda walked into Mr. Tate's office, he said, "You and I need to talk about Gloria." She settled herself in a comfortable chair across from Mr. Tate's desk and he began by saying, "It is my fault alone and I should have mentioned it before but Gloria will not be with us very long, maybe a year. It was the Langleys' wishes she be enrolled in a private school in Switzerland which they did about two months before their terrible accident. That is what they wanted from the courts papers and I will be abiding by that decision. Of course, they left Gloria financially secure and at twenty-one, she will be a very rich young lady. That is the main reason the relatives from Mississippi wanted to take her back there to live. I have to think of Gloria's future, so therefore when she goes to Switzerland, I would like for you to accompany her when I am notified for her to enter. I am hoping that you are happy in your position here because I need your help to accomplish what has to be done relative to Gloria. So, please let me know if there is anything that I or Regis can do to help you. Also, here is a check to cover the expense of the piano. It was a wonderful gesture but it should not be your expense. Thanks so much for the great work you have been doing."

After leaving Mr. Tate, Hilda proceeded upstairs to her living area. Ascending the staircase, she heard the faint tones of a piano which stopped her in her tracks. The music was beautiful and she thought could this be Gloria. She moved further up the staircase toward the small room where Regis said the piano had been moved during last evening. She didn't open the door to the room but stood outside listening to the beautiful music. She almost broke down crying but she knew that would not be the right thing to do. Opening the door, she saw Gloria, her face shining as never before, playing her heart out.

Hilda went over and hugged her saying, "Well, I know what you enjoy doing. You don't need to tell me how much you like the piano that I bought for you."

Gloria kept playing without even using any music, just pieces that she had memorized it seemed. Hilda noticed that there were sheets of music on top of the piano that Gloria must have brought with her when she arrived.

Gloria smiled at Hilda, saying, "Did you buy the piano just for me? Don't you play? I'm most happy when I am at the piano. I want it to be part of my life when I grow up. My mother and father told me that I could play well for my age. Thanks so much for getting me the piano."

Hilda thought of her mother eventhough she had been dead for years. She still remembered her Poppa saying how well she played the organ. She thought, well, maybe her granddaughter received some of this talent. She excused herself going to her room to have a good cry.

In the afternoon, Regis and Hilda took Maxine and Gloria for a drive. They stopped at the park and while sitting around, Hilda observed both of them. Maxine was running around acting her age and having fun while Gloria was more reserved and intent on what was happening around her. She acted much older than her eleven years. Hilda thought, if she keeps improving her music from what she heard today, she will be great.

Also, going through her mind was, "Will I ever be able to tell her that I am her real mother? I will miss this child when she leaves for school in Europe."

The first thing that Gloria did when they arrived back at the complex was to proceed to the music room as she called it. She stayed in there until Mrs. Styne took her and Maxine down for supper.

At supper time, Regis told Hilda that Mr. Tate wanted to see her later. She wondered what he wanted to say. She asked Regis if he knew what he wanted but told her that he didn't have a clue. She told Regis that she heard Gloria play the piano and she could hardly believe how she performed.

Quickly, he said, "I would love to hear her. Do you think we could do this later?"

"I don't see why not after I see what Mr. Tate has to say. I will call you when the coast is clear," commented Hilda.

Leaving Regis, she proceeded to Mr. Tate's office, hoping he would be there and he was waiting for her.

Entering the office, she sat in her ususal spot. She noticed that he had some papers in his hand. He leaned back and stared a moment. smiling, saying, "Young lady, it looks like you are going to be a traveler pretty soon. I have these papers, in my hand which just arrived yesterday, confirmation of Gloria's acceptance in the Arts School of Switzerland. They have accepted her even though she is only a few months from being twelve years of age. This would have pleased the Langleys because they loved this child so much. Everything they owned, the houses here, in Florida, and one in France, will be hers one day. She is a very lucky child in this way but it is sad to think about her not having someone to love her in a parental way. I want you to accompany her to this school, enroll her and take care of whatever is necessary. I know I can depend on you. The sky is the limit, everything will be taken care of by her estate. I don't want you to feel that I am putting pressure on you to do this. I want you to feel comfortable because I know you are capable. I have observed you from the very first time that I laid eyes upon you and feel very secure in saying what I have told you."

CHAPTER SIXTEEN

Hilda's head was now twirling inside. This was a big undertaking, could she do it, of course, this was her child. She braced her back, looking straight into Mr. Tate's eyes, she said, "I will do what is best for Gloria, treating her as if she were mine. If I run into any difficulties, I will call on you for guidance, is that a deal."

Smiling, Mr. Tate stood up, extending his hand, saying, "That's a deal and I am at you beck and call when it comes to the child. Start preparing for a departure in about 30 days. I will take care of everything you both will need, just be ready to travel when I give you the date." Laughing, he said, "The piano stays for her when she comes back for visits. I heard her play and she really has the talent. We have lots to look forward to as she grows older."

Back in her room, so many thoughts were running through her mind. She want be able to see Gloria very often, maybe twice a year, if lucky. Should she divulge to Mr. Tate anything relative to her being Gloria's real mother. I told him that I would look after her as if she were mine, so that should be enough at this moment but there would be a time when she promised herself that she would reveal herself to Gloria.

Hearing the tinkling of the piano, she remembered that she had told Regis that as soon as she was free that she would call him. He wanted to hear Gloria play the piano. Using the house phone, she called Regis and he told her that he would be there in a flash.

A knock appeared at her door, it seems as quickly as she put down the phone. In the hallway, both Regis and Hilda listened to the music swirling out from under the door of the music room. Hilda was glad that Regis had the piano delivered to that little room which Gloria now called the music room.

Regis was in awe as to the quality of the performance without seeing the performer. As Hilda opened the door to the room, they positioned themselves into chairs nearby but all the commotion didn't seem to bother Gloria because she kept on playing as if she was in a world of her own. She played without ceasing one piece right after the other which I am sure she had memorized.

After listening for awhile, Hilda went over to her and said, "Gloria, Mr. Regis wanted to hear you play. Your playing is unbelievable and I am so proud of you."

Regis said, "Gloria how long have you been taking lessons. You play so beautifully and I noticed your sheet music on top of the piano which is for adults."

Gloria replied quickly, "I have been in training since I was 4 years old. I got bored with the music that I had to learn at first but when they found out I could play the more difficult pieces, they let me. When I started they had to have a special piano for me because it was difficult for me to reach the keys but now my hands have grown long and I have no trouble at all." She stretched out her hands for Regis to observe. For a child of nearly twelve, she did have big hands, almost adult size.

Regis said to Hilda, "She talks and acts like a person several years older than twelve and her music is adult music. Just think how good she is going to be with more training as she says. Mr. Tate told me today about talking to you about going with her to Switzerland to enroll her at the Arts School.

He said it could be possible within the next thirty days. You know I am going to miss you because I imagine you will be gone a couple of weeks or more."

Hilda looked straight into his deep, blue eyes, saying, "As much as we like each other, but with your plans of going to New York to try the audition route for awhile and me headed for Europe, I don't see any romantic plans for us in the near future."

The look on Regis' face was that of a rejected child to Hilda but he said, "I haven't spoken to Mr. Tate about spending a month in New York but while you were gone would be a great time to go.

You gave me a good idea to see if I could do it while you are away. I am going to talk with him about it."

"Do you need a loan to help finance your stay in New York, if so, you are welcome to the $5,000 check returned by Mr. Tate," commented Hilda.

"Your really mean that, I can tell by the your body language," Regis quickly retorted.

Hilda stared at him for a moment, saying, "I have really loved only three men in my life, my Poppa, high school sweetheart, Anthony Leo, and now you. When I first met you, I felt that I would never be able to experience love again, but I have become very fond of you."

Regis reached over and took her hand in his, and with a very caressing look said, "I am not worthy of your love because I have been around the world and back relative to romance, in reality, I am telling you that I have been around all kinds of people in my short life and have experienced the fruits thereof. I am not bragging because it has been very difficult for me to tell the good from the bad. But, since I have met you, I see the good things I have been missing. Thanks for the offer of the loan, who knows, I may talk with you later about it, if Mr. Tate will give me a month off."

As Hilda left to see about the children, she said to Regis, "Whatever you decide. Will see you at dinner."

Hilda decided that she would spruce up a bit for dinner after having a short nap. While dressing, she wondered why everything had seemed so nice and quiet. Probably, Miss Booth had both Maxine and Gloria under control. She was very firm and had a direct approach when around them. They seemed to like her very much. Hilda knew her position was too confining to be in charge of the children on a day to day basis. Her position now was on the order of an executive assistant, not as a nanny as originally employed. She was so glad that Mr. Tate had employed just the right women to handle the situation.

Within three weeks, Hilda was on her way with Gloria to enroll her in the Art School in Lucerne, Switzerland. Regis had permission from Mr. Tate to try his luck on the Broadway audition circuit and had been there a week with a full schedule as he had notified Hilda before leaving for Europe. It took a full three weeks before Hilda returned to the Tate Compound. Upon her arrival back, Mr. Tate notified her that Regis had been given a supporting role in a drama headed for Broadway in a couple of months but was now in rehearsals. Hilda was so happy that Regis would be doing something that he really wanted to do. She felt that this incident would lead to bigger and better roles, maybe the movies.

While talking with Mr. Tate, she gave him a run-down on the Art School and Gloria. Gloria was very satisfied and happy but she wanted me to return for a week's visit after a three-month period. This had been suggested by the Director of the school.

Mr. Tate said, "Of course, you will follow up on this situation and conduct yourself accordingly.

This whole situation is in your hands. Just let me know when you plan to be away. Her estate will take care of all expenses. Also, by the way, Regis has an old friend, who is going to take his place. He just arrived from England the week before you came back from Switzerland. He will be at dinner tonight and will be at Regis' table."

With a hint of a smile, he winked, saying, "He looks younger than Regis," as he excused himself.

Hilda proceeded upstairs to get ready to meet the new chauffeur at dinner. She had an hour before making an appearance. After dressing, she sat down and her mind was going from one thing to another. First, she wondered how the new chauffeur would be, would he be as nice as Regis? Would she be going to check on Gloria more than once or twice a year? Would her position at the Tate Compound develop into something completely different than as a Nanny. She loved what was going on but her contact with the children was something that she missed. Now, she might not see Gloria very often and that bothered her.

Anyway, she had been back from D'Lo for almost two years and felt like she should make a quick trip home to see if Jerlene was doing ok in her situation. This had to be her next project and after dinner she was going to talk with Mr. Tate about a quick trip home for two or three days. She would not let Jerlene know that she was coming, just make a surprise visit, maybe rent a car when she gets to Meridian.

She got up from her rest, knowing full well that she had to be at dinner to meet the new chauffeur. As she walked into the dining area and looking toward Regis' table, a gentleman stood up and waited for her to be seated.

He said, "I am Jarvis Stuart, Regis' friend, from London. Mr. Tate gave me his position, since Regis is now in the theatre. Regis couldn't say enough good things about you and I believe them now since I have met you. Let's have a glass of wine on our future friendship."

All agog, looking at Jarvis, Hilda was overwhelmed as to how much he favored Regis. She said, "You two look so much alike, could you be kin?

Jarvis quickly said, "We have heard that many times before, especially in Europe. Of course, I think I am more handsome that Regis."

They talked for quite awhile and then he said, "I have to meet with Mr. Tate for a spell but will see you later. I am to be at your disposal at all times, so I am told by Regis and Mr. Tate. Nice meeting you and thanks for the good dinner conversation."

Hilda passed by Mr. Tate's office on her way from dinner and noticed that Jarvis, the new chauffeur, was having a conversation with him. Mr. Tate waved, motioning for her to come inside. Upon entering his office, Mr. Tate said, "Have a seat and we'll have a chat."

After talking awhile, Jarvis said, "I'll see you both later." Looking at Hilda, he reiterated saying, "I'm at your beck and call."

Before leaving, Hilda asked Mr. Tate if she could do a quick trip home to Mississippi. He approved and told her if she needed anything to let him know. He told her to let Miss Booth and Miss Spikes know that she would be away for a few days.

Hilda finally got everything in order and reserved an air flight direct Jackson and then would rent a car because she wanted to surprise Jerlene.

The next couple of days were hectic for Hilda but she finally was set for her trip and told Jarvis she would like for him to take her to the airport. She left Boston at 7: a,m, and didn't arrive in Jackson until 2: p.m. because she had a lay over in DC which she was not counting on.

Arriving at the Jackson Airport, she inquired about a rental car and they handled it immediately and she was off to D'Lo. As she drove into North D'Lo, she noticed that the old school house had been torn down which she could see as she turned into the driveway of her home. Why would anyone want to demolish that beautiful old building? It could have been used for a town museum or city hall. It was difficult to realize that she first left her beloved D'Lo almost ten years ago. She wondered if she would ever return to stay and at one time that was what she really wanted.

As she parked the car, Jerlene was not in sight but after getting out of the car, she heard someone laughing and hollering, "Oh!, Ms Hilda, is that you? You have been away for two whole years. I am so happy to see you. Come on in and let's have a glass of tea."

Hilda looked at Jerlene and she looked better than she did at her Poppa's funeral. Hilda asked her if everything was alright.

Jerlene said, "Ms Hilda, look around and tell me what you think."

Hilda couldn't find anything to complain about and was actually surprised that the house and grounds looked beautiful. So, she said to Jerlene "I had to have a break, so I decided to just drop in to see how you were. I can only stay around for a couple of days."

"Well, in that case, I will cook up some good food for you and we can talk about our good times," said Jerlene.

Hilda said, "Wonderful and I can tell you all about what I have been doing and where I've been. Since Poppa's funeral, I have been to Switzerland. I do have a great position with this wealthy family."

"We'll have a good supper and then move to the veranda and talk," commented Jerlene.

Jerlene left going to the kitchen and Hilda went to her old bedroom. Upon entering, memories of the past overwhelmed her and she fell across the oversized bed and cried like a baby.

On the back veranda, Jerlene had sat up everything just like having a party. Much good food was abound, with a pitcher of mint juleps on a table nearby. They sat there for almost three hours drinking and eating when several people arrived calling for Jerlene.

Hilda didn't understand what was happening until she heard one big, black guy say, "Jerlene, honey, am I gonna stay with you tonight?

Hilda glanced at Jerlene. The expression on her face was a picture of guilt that could not be denied. Jerlene dropped her head and said, "Ms Hilda, I can not lie to you because you have been so good to me."

Immediately, Hilda said, "Jerlene, this is your affair but don't be using the house to cater to acts of this sort. You do understand, because people in D'Lo will be talking and won't approve. When I go into D'Lo tomorrow, someone, I am sure will tell me about it, if you have been doing this on a regular basis."

Jerlene said, "Ms Hilda, I am sorry and I promise to end this type of shenanigan. I don't want these high-falutin white folks in D'Lo to criticize you. So don't you worry you pretty little head again."

Jerlene noticed that everyone left when they saw she had someone with her.

Hilda said, "I am a bit tired, so I am going to bed and we'll talk more tomorrow."

Lying in bed, she wondered if Jerlene had been using the house for her affairs with some of the men in D'Lo. Maybe she could find out more in the next couple of days.

Waking up, the sun was shining into her room and reminded her of past experiences. She kept thinking as she dressed casually, some of the best days of her life was in this very house.

Jerlene had breakfast on the veranda table and as she sat down, voices came from the front of the house. Two white guys, who looked familiar to Hilda came walking through the house calling for Jerlene.

Jerlene stood up by the table, saying, "Max, you and Carl come on out on the veranda and see Ms Hilda. She is back home for a visit."

As they both approached, "Max said, "Hilda Webber, Carl and I haven't seen you in several years, not since high school. You were pretty then but now you have really become a raving beauty. Anthony Leo, your beau back then, always talked about you and bragging that he was going to marry you. When yo'all broke up, it nearly drove him crazy. By the way, did you know that he was killed in a bad auto accident, not too long before the family moved back to Pennsylvania?

Hilda noticed these two handsome men, from well to do families, who were her class mates had not changed one iota, blue jeans, cowboy boots, chevrolet convertibles, and money in their pockets.

Hilda hugged them both and said, "What brings you over here to my house?"

Carl said, "Jerlene launders our jeans and shirts because we don't like how they do'em at the cleaners. We pay Jerlene twice as much as the laundry charges but they are like we want'em. She does a great job."

By that time, Jerlene came forth holding two big bundles of shirts and jeans on wire hangers. She said, "Here you are big guys, just lay the money over there on the table."

As they left, both reached over and almost hugged Jerlene, Max said, "Hilda, it was a nice surprise seeing you after all these years. Whatever you are doing, must agree with you because you look good to me. Too bad you are not going to be around awhile, we might have been able to see each other."

Hilda laughed a bit, saying, "Max, I have a good position and don't want to jeopardize it but thanks anyway."

Carl chimed in saying, "Hilda, you know that you don't have to work because I have heard the rumor that your Dad left you with plenty of money."

Quickly she said, "I had a good Poppa but don't always believe rumors. By the way, what are you two guys doing with your lives?"

Carl said, "I'm working with my Dad and so is Max, otherwise life goes on."

As the two guys pulled out of the driveway in a bright yellow convertible, Hilda wondered if Jerlene was having affairs with her high school classmates.

After two days, Hilda had to return to Boston. Before leaving she did not say anything more to Jerlene about what she might be doing because the place was immaculate, actually beautiful. Even, Jerlene looked happy.

Returning back to the Tate Compound, she had to make a quick trip back to Switzerland because the director had requested an in-person seminar relative to each student.

When she returned from Switzerland, Mr. Tate sent her to one of his condominiums in Puerto Rico because he felt that she needed a vacation. He told her that she had been working too hard and not enough time off.

On the way to Puerto Rico, she stopped off in New York and spent two days with Regis. He told her how happy he was with his acting career. She went to one of his rehearsal and she knew then that he was going to be well known one of these days, maybe after the play opens in the fall on Broadway.

She stayed in Puerto Rico for ten days and on her way back she stopped for another interlude with Regis. Regis tried to get serious with her by asking her to quit her job and come live with him in New York. Hilda told him that at this time, she had committed herself to the children and Mr. Tate depended on her so much. He agreed with her but made her promise to come to New York whenever possible.

Hilda got back in the groove at the Tate Compound and everything went along very smoothly. Jarvis was just as helpful as Regis and was always wanting to take her out or go somewhere in the evening.

Months went by not seeing Mr. Tate but he would always call and talk, actually not saying where he was. He would always end by saying, "Jarvis knows how to contact me if you need me. Thanks, you are doing an excellent job."

Sitting in her room one night, she started taking inventory. Just think, Regis is on Broadway and the media is proclaiming him a new star on the horizon. I have been to D'Lo three times in the last six years and all seems to be doing fine there. I have been to Switzerland close to twenty-five times in the last six years, checking on Gloria who is now approaching seventeen. She is doing great in her music world being acclaimed a talented child protege. Her next phase will be the concert stage starting in Russia within the next year. But, to Hilda something was missing and that was, as yet she had not divulged to any one that Gloria was her own flesh and blood. She wondered how Gloria would react when she was told. Would she be happy or would she reject her for not telling her sooner. She was at her wits end, thinking of her being in her middle forties but before she talked with Mr. Tate regarding Gloria, she was going to see how Gloria did at the beginning of her concert performances.

The year passed and as Hilda predicted, Regis was now being courted for other Broadway plays and even a movie. Gloria won national acclaim from her concert on the Russian circuit and was now coming to New York to play at Carnegie Hall, then maybe a world tour. According to Hilda's feelings, she felt she had held back long enough relative to Gloria, so she made up her mind that she would talk with Mr. Tate when he arrived back from a trip to Paris with friends.

She read most of the next day, it seemed to relax her. Jarvis talked about his day and also mentioned that Mr. Tate called and would be home the next day.

Hearing that Mr. Tate's arrival was imminent, it sent Hilda's mind into a spin. She must get her thoughts together on how to approach him concerning Gloria. Her mind had been made up relative to Gloria even if it meant her demise from the Tate Compound.

The next day upon arrival of Mr. Tate, Hilda received a call from him asking her to come to the office as he wanted to talk with her. She wondered, as she slowly walked down the stairs to his office, what in the world did he want to discuss with her.

Upon entering his office, he seemed to have a sad look on his face. Hilda said, "Mr. Tate are you feeling well today?"

Mr. Tate replied, "I don't feel my usual self today because of food-poisoning. I ate something that didn't agree with me and had to have a doctor. But, I think I am on the mend, I hope so anyway."

Mr. Tate sat back in his overstuffed chair staring at Hilda for a moment. He said, "Hilda, it seems that Gloria is going to need a chaperone for her concert tours which have been booked for the next four or five years. I think that you would be the right candidate for this position. At the end of these tours, she will be twenty-one and legally on her own.

What she will do after she becomes of age, no one knows but she will be financially secure to do as she wishes. What do you think of the situation?"

Hilda looked down at her purse which she made sure that she brought. Opening it up, fumbling around to get the birth certificate, pulling it out and laid in her lap. She said, "Mr. Tate, I have not been very truthful with you relative to why I am in your employ. Ever since I left my home in D'Lo, I have been trying to work my way toward Hartford, Connecticut because of a baby. That baby is Gloria who was adopted by Mr. and Mrs. Jason Jackson Langley. I wanted to be near her and had thoughts at one time that there might be a chance to work for them so I could be near her and watch her grow up.

Here is Gloria's birth certificate that shows that I am her real mother. When I was fifteen, just out of high school, I was raped by someone and my father sent me to an unwed mother's home in Natchez, Mississippi where Gloria was born. The Langleys adopted her from that home."

Mr. Tate's eyes looked big as cups with water, staring at Hilda. He dropped his head and raised it saying, "Hilda, what misery you have must have gone through keeping all of this to yourself and not being able to share with anyone. What kind of reaction is going to happen when you tell Gloria, because you are going to tell her? I believe that she is at the age that she might just understand. You know she will be here next week to begin preparation for her Carnegie Hall Concert. Together we'll have a talk with her and see what happens. By the way, I understand now why you bought that piano. I wondered how you could have afforded it."

Hilda said, "I jumped at the chance to do something that I knew she enjoyed, her music. The money was no problem as my Dad left me secure. I loved the position here because it meant being nearer my baby, Gloria. It has been difficult at times for me. I hope that revealing my secret doesn't jeopardize our relationship."

CHAPTER SEVENTEEN

Mr. Tate said, "First, we must think of Gloria and what repercussion it will have on her life right at this moment when she is at the height of her future career. As for you and me, I understand and sympathize with your situation. I will still help you in anyway that will make you and Gloria's relationship one that will be advantageous to both of you. I still say that you have really been carrying around a huge burden. I do hope that you feel better after talking with me. As soon as Gloria arrives on Monday, we three will have a talk."

Hilda's week-end wasn't too bad because she felt more relieved after her talk with Mr. Tate. But, she wondered just how Gloria would react when she was told, after all she's nearly seventeen.

Late Monday afternoon, Gloria arrived and was inquiring the whereabout of Maxine as she had a gift for her that she purchased in Russia. She was told that she was away at boarding school in Maine. Maxine and Gloria didn't really have much rapport because Gloria was older and acted more mature. Mrs. Styne told her that she would be home for the summer soon and that seemed to please Gloria.

Mr. Tate phoned Hilda and told her that after dinner they would have a talk including Gloria. Hilda was glad things were coming to a head, at least get it off her conscience. It had been a bottled up secret long enough.

Having dinner with Jarvis was a joy because he kept her laughing. She knew that was good for her right at this time. He would talk about the difference between American and English habits and laugh along with her.

After dinner, Hilda walked toward Mr. Tate's office and she could see that Gloria was already there talking with him. Hilda stared through the big window and noticed how beautiful and poised she was at sixteen. She could actually see some features that reminded her of the only young picture available of her Mother. Gloria got her looks and talent from her.

As she walked into Mr. Tate's office, Gloria raised from her chair and came toward Hilda and hugged her, saying, Miss Hilda I have missed you so much."

Hilda noticed the big smile that came across Mr. Tate's face as she was greeted by Gloria. She was hoping that it was a good omen of things to come.

After all were seated comfortably, Mr. Tate got up and locked the door so no one would be able to disturb them. He looked directly at Gloria saying, "Gloria, I know the Langleys told you several years ago that you had been adopted from a home in Mississippi. Did they ever mention anything about your Mother, whether she was dead or living? From what they told me that was never discussed but since you are a young lady going on seventeen, I think that we are at a stage in your life that this could be discussed."

Gloria looked a little puzzled, wondering why this was being discussed now. But she answered Mr. Tate saying, "Yes, they told me about my adoption and how blessed they were to have me. I believed they loved me because they were so good to me. Why do we have to talk about my adoption?"

Immediately, Mr. Tate said, "Gloria, Ms Hilda has something to say to you. At first, you might not believe what you will be hearing but my attorneys have checked it all out the last several weeks and it is all true. So listen to what she has to say."

Hilda looked straight at Gloria, as she began saying, "Long time ago when I was fifteen, a year younger than you, I was raped and my Father sent me to a home in Natchez, Mississippi to have my baby. I knew that I was too young and inexperienced to raise my child and no Mother to help me, so I let them put my baby up for adoption. They would not tell me because of legal reasons who adopted my child but I went back to the home and worked awhile hoping to find out. I did volunteer work there and going through some records, I found out that my baby had been adopted by Mr.

and Mrs. Jason Langley of Hartford, Connecticut. After three or four years, I couldn't stand it any longer so I proceeded to move toward where my baby was living. Then, with the permission of my father, I came to New York hoping to find a nanny position with the idea of moving closer to Hartford. I was interviewed in New York for a position with Mr. Tate and here I am. Do you understand what I am trying to tell you?

Gloria moved from her chair crying and into the arms of Hilda saying, "Are you my real Mother. I hoped one day that this would happen. It is hard to believe and yet I wonder why you haven't told me before now. I have been here for almost five years and you haven't said a word. It makes me believe that you had doubts as to whether I would love you or not. You are my real Mother, of course, I care for you. I loved you from the first day that I arrived here from Hartford because of the way you treated me. Your love shone through the day you bought that piano just for me."

All three were standing, Mr. Tate, Hilda and Gloria, with their arms around each other. For now everything seem to be going well, surmised Mr. Tate.

He said, "We'll talk more later but as for now I have some other business to take care before going to bed."

Hilda and Gloria left hand in hand toward the music room. Gloria played a long time causing, Mrs. Styne, Ms Booth and Jarvis to join them. Upon finishing, Gloria said, "Before anyone leaves, I would like to make an announcement to everyone."

All were stunned as she said, "This has been a wonderful day for me. I would like to introduce to you, my real Mother, Ms. Hilda."

Everyone was confused with much hugging and laughing but no questions came forth. Hilda was very surprised that no one questioned her. Gloria's actions were that of a nice, little lady of sweet sixteen.

Hilda knew that Gloria had an independent attitude, so she let her think she was making most decisions herself. Gloria even discussed with her that Mr. Tate had said that she would be her chaperone on the tours coming up. Everything seemed to be going well and it made Hilda much more relaxed than usual.

Gloria's performance at Carnegie Hall was a sellout. The media was good to her with rave reviews. Mr. Tate settled everything with the company who was handling her concert tours and she was off with Hilda to play in the major U.S. cities then to the Orient and Europe.

After being on the tour for about two years, Hilda and Gloria returned to the Tate Compound for a planned rest in Orlando, Florida. Mr. Tate sent them to a condominium that the Langleys had willed to Gloria. Hilda was tired of traveling so she really enjoyed the Florida vacation and she got to know Gloria better.

As yet Gloria had not started or even mentioned the dating situation. She did have men to call her but were just acquaintances met at concerts. Hilda wondered how long this would go on before there would be someone special in her life. Gloria was very good to Hilda and at times called her Mother. Hilda was thankful that she had a good relationship with her even though it wasn't really like Mother and daughter. Hilda would say to herself, after all I wasn't with her in her early years, just be thankful for being here.

Back at the Tate Compound after vacationing in Florida, Hilda called Jerlene and everything was doing fine in D'Lo.

The next two years of concert went fast and Gloria and Hilda returned to the Tate Compound for a much needed rest. Mr Tate told them he wanted to have a talk. Hilda felt that it was relative to Gloria becoming twenty-one years of age.

Jarvis called Hilda asking to meet him for dinner. Hilda told him that she was bringing Gloria with her. They all had a great time and Gloria seemed more relaxed than Hilda had ever seen. Jarvis asked her lots of questions about her career. She seemed to be happy answering him because Gloria was happy with what she was doing. Hilda saw another side of Gloria that she had never seen before. It really pleased Hilda so much.

Mr. Tate came by and told Hilda and Gloria to meet him in the office when they were finished.

When Hilda and Gloria arrived in Mr. Tate's office, he jumped up hugging Gloria saying, "Happy Birthday, tomorrow you will be twenty-one."

Just about the time Mr. Tate was hugging Gloria, a man appeared at the door of Mr. Tate's office. Mr. Tate said, "Gloria, this is Lawyer Eskell, who will tell you what to expect when the Langley will is probated in court next week."

Gloria smiled saying, "Well, I know they were very good to me and I loved them dearly. Mrs. Langley and I would go to the condo in Orlando certain times of the year and she would always say to me this will be one of your homes some day. Miss Hilda and I just had a lovely vacation there. I really hope that I can begin living there when I am not on concert tour."

Mr. Eskell began by reading the will for the purpose of getting Gloria familiar what would be read to her next week at probate court. It stated that she would get a lump sum of money which was already in the bank, plus the house in Hartford, a house in Madrid, Spain and the condo in Orlando. She would be able to spend a certain amount of the money each year until she became twenty-five years of age, then she could make her own decisions.

After reading of the will, the lawyer asked her if she understood. Gloria said, "Yes, I understand it all. I am so happy about the condo in Orlando because I plan to make it my home where I can come and rest after my concerts. I really plan to live there after the probation of the will. I feel that I am capable of living on my own and my concert manager will take care of my business."

Mr. Tate gazed over at Hilda and he noticed the sad look on her face. After all Gloria was twenty-one and legally she was in charge of her life which she stated that was the way she desired it to be.

Mr. Eskell handed a copy of the will to Mr. Tate and shook his hand as he left. "After the reading of the will next week, Gloria would be given a copy," said Mr. Tate.

Mr. Tate bade the lawyer goodbye and then turned around to Hilda and Gloria saying, "Let's all have a glass of wine to Gloria's birthday."

Gloria laughed saying, "It will be my first glass ever, so let's do it. Who knows I might like it. I appreciate everyone being so nice to me. Miss Hilda you are going to be a super Mom."

Hilda turned around to look at her, tears brimming from her eyes, hugged her and kissed her on the cheek.

Gloria said, "I'm going up stairs and play awhile. When I get too emotional, I head for the piano and it soothes my nerves. See all of you later."

Hilda and Mr Tate stood there looking at each other after Gloria left, not saying a word. Words were not appropriate because they understood each other.

As Hilda proceeded toward the music room, she could hear Gloria playing one tune right after the other. They were happy tunes, so she must be happy.

Hilda felt better today more than she had in a long time. It seemed everything was falling into place. It really didn't matter where Gloria lives as long as she recognizes me as her Mother and I could see her sometime.

Hilda had a feeling that Gloria wanted to live alone and that was fine if she showed her that she could cope with the situation. Gloria was smart and very meticulous in every way. How she would handle a bank account is another question. She would find out in the next few weeks because they would be going back to Orlando after probate court.

Mr. Tate had already informed her that Gloria informed him that she wanted to move to Orlando and wanted a live in maid-servant. Hilda thought since she had missed being with her in the earlier years that was all fine and dandy with her as long as she had good rapport and could see her when she felt like it. Anyway, she would just wait and see how the scenario played out.

The next week rolled around and on Tuesday, Mr. Tate was informed to bring Gloria to Judge Wilson's office in downtown Hartford. Hilda was asked by Mr. Tate to accompany them.

As they approached the judge's chambers, he said, "Gloria Langley, would you please sit over here to my left."

She seemed so poised and ladylike as she took her seat as directed. She turned around and smiled at both Hilda and Mr. Tate. Sitting there with her arms crossed with her hands in her lap, she seemed to be in control of herself. Hilda really noticed today how much she really favored her grandmother Webber. To her it was a great feeling to just gaze upon her and think about what she had accomplished in her life at the young age of twenty-one. She thought if she had stayed in D'Lo, would she have been the same person that she is today.

Judge Wilson looked around and noticed that there was a couple sitting in the back and he inquired as to why. He was told that they were relatives of the Langleys who were asked to be in attendance for the reading of the will. He asked them to join Mr. Tate and Hilda. They came forward and introduced themselves as Mr. and Mrs. Bud Lambert of Greenville, Mississippi.

With everyone seated, the Judge began by saying, "We are here today to probate the will of Mr. and Mrs. Jason Jackson Langley. They left an heir, a daughter, Gloria Langley. As he read, he pointed to her, saying, "Gloria Langley you are the adopted daughter of Mr. and Mrs. Jason Jackson Langley and it hereby states that you are the sole heir. Since you have become twenty-one years of age, you are recipient of everything owned by them. I will give you a copy of the will and you can read what is stipulated to be in your possession. Also, you will receive a yearly allowance of $100,000 dollars for the next five years beginning the first of the month, which will be pro-rated for the remainder of this year.

After the first five years, you will be in charge of all your finances henceforth.

Also, Mrs. Bud Lambert, maiden name, Lila Langley, sister of Mr. Jason Jackson Langley is bequeathed an amount of $200,000.00. This will be mailed to her by the Mr. Tate, executor of Mr. and Mrs. Langley's will.

Gloria remembered right after the accident, five years ago, that they showed up on the scene wanting to take her home with them to Mississippi. Mr. Tate would not let them because he had been designated as her guardian in the Langley will. They left in a huff and had not been heard of since then only rumors that they were going to sue for her custody.

After the meeting with the judge, Mr. Tate asked that everyone remain for a short while. He went forward and handed a paper to Judge Wilson and conferred with him for a few minutes.

The judge cleared his throat and looked straight at Hilda, saying, "Would you come up to my podium, I have something to say to everyone."

He asked Hilda to turn around and face everyone, saying, "One of the most wonderful things have been told to me today and after analyzing the proof which I have in my hand, it must be a miracle.

This lady known as Hilda Webber is the real mother of this young lady, Gloria Langley. She has been employed by Mr. Tate for a long time and has kept this a secret within her heart for years. Just think how difficult this must have been. This is a great day for the both of them. It is wonderful to know that she has a real biological family. Also, this should be a warning to anyone that might want to bring any type of legal action against this young lady or her estate."

Mr. Tate noticed as the Lamberts left the judge's chambers that they didn't look too pleased after the judge's remarks.

Hilda thought to herself as usual, I'll think about that tomorrow.

On the way back to the Tate Compound, Mr. Tate asked that Hilda and Gloria have dinner with him. Hilda thought this may be a fun evening, wondering if Jarvis would be present.

The very first thing that Gloria did upon arriving at the compound was find her way to the piano. Hilda could hear her playing as if she were doing a concert.

At dinner that night, everyone was having a joyous evening. Jarvis showed up and Hilda was glad that he could spend some time with everyone. Gloria told everyone that she would be leaving for Orlando on the week-end and invited Hilda to accompany her.

Hilda was very excited about going back to Florida for a vacation before Gloria left on her concert tour. Before she and Gloria left, Mr. Tate had talked to her concerning Gloria, saying, "She has asked for a live-in maid to be with her on her next tours. But, just be patient and everything will work out. She is doing her best to accept you as a Mother because she has talked with me about you. She loves you and wants you to be a part of her life. How much, that remains to be seen. Always be available for her and tell her so. I am not going to question you relative to your past because you have proven to me to be a very reputable person. Anyway, all of us have skeletons in our closet. You can always depend on me if I can be of assistance. As you know, Maxine is finishing high school and will be going to a private college. I feel very sad to say, so with Gloria and Maxine both gone, I will not have a legitimate reason for you to stay in my employ. Mrs. Styne will remain here as a supervisor-housekeeper.

Sitting in her room, Hilda began to reflect back to the time she first came to the Tate Compound. It was difficult to believe that she had been away from D'Lo twenty-five years. I was twenty-five years of age at the time and I thought that surely I would be married by this time. Tears swelled up in her eyes with the thought of being able to see her baby at most any time now. Hilda felt blessed because really that was the uppermost idea in her mind at the time. She felt that she had accomplished what she had set out to do.

A knock on her door, brought Hilda to reality. As she looked around, it was Gloria, smiling and seemed so happy.

She said, "Mother, I am looking forward to us having a good rest in Orlando. Mr. Tate informed me that he had contacted an agency and we should have a live-in maid when we arrive. That will be fine and if we don't like her then we can secure another."

Hilda walked over and hugged her, saying, "I know that we will enjoy each other and remember to let me know if I can do anything to help out, that's what I am here for. I want you to make your own decisions but remember I am here for you, if needed.

Gloria seemed pleased after their talk and left, saying, "Plane reservations are for 7: a.m. Saturday."

As Hilda prepared for bed she could hear Gloria playing the piano. Lying in bed, she wondered about Gloria and the Tate

Compound. She didn't like living here and Hilda felt that she would permanently move to Florida, probably this would be the time.

The week-end came, Gloria and Hilda were off to Florida. Gloria seemed in hyper heaven as their plane headed toward her home in Orlando.

Upon arrival, Hilda saw that Mr. Tate had everything planned, new live-in maid, and a limousine at their disposal. Hilda didn't take over the rein of making decisions, she let Gloria do it, after all it was her home.

Gloria took charge just as if she had been doing it all the time. She asked the new maid, Angie, who was from Ireland to come into her office.

Hilda didn't want to interfere, so she said to Gloria, "I am going to start unpacking and hanging up my clothes."

Gloria looked perturbed, saying, "That is going to be a part of the maid's duties, so just hold on for awhile until I have time to go over her duties. You need to rest awhile and then we'll check out the rest of the house later.

Hilda shook her head affirmatively and went toward the huge den which Gloria loved. It had built in everything with a huge, black, grand piano. Hilda thought, surely she wants to live here permanently with everything a person could want.

Within an hour, Gloria joined Hilda in the den, saying, "Angie will bring us a cool drink in a short while. She is just what this house needs, someone to wait on us. If they can't do what I ask them to do, then they can just get out. Mother, I bet you had someone back in your Mississippi home that waited on you hand and foot."

Hilda saw a side to Gloria that she had hidden for sometime. Mrs. Langley spoiled her to the point that she probably thinks she is better than some folks. That will be one thing that I will work on in the coming weeks, thought Hilda.

Thinking about her sweet maid, Jerlene, she said, "I must confess that my maid, Jerlene, did it all, wonderful cook, cleaning that big, old house, keeping everything up to par even to helping me dress, lying out my clothes, even telling me what I should be wearing. Of course, she adored my father and waited upon him until his death not too many years ago. After his death, I left her as caretaker of my home and she could live there the rest of her life. Sometime I would like for her to visit us here or us visit my home in D'Lo. Of course, she doesn't know anything about you being my daughter. I feel that you and Jerlene would like each other very much."

Gloria immediately said, "Why doesn't she know about you and me?

"As soon as I knew that I was pregnant, I left for an unwed mother's home in Natchez and stayed there and did volunteer work until your were born. She was never made aware that I had a beautiful, baby girl," said Hilda.

"If she did visit us would she inquire if I called you, Mother? I don't want to cause any dissension among us. I want everything to be happy and gay, just like my life, thanks to you."

"She probably wouldn't think anything, knowing Jerlene's temperament. Probably, giggle some because she loves to laugh and giggle, like a younger person than she is," reiterated Hilda.

After a few weeks, Gloria and Hilda hit the road on concert tour throughout the USA and then to England and Europe. The next three years, Hilda was well indoctrinated with people whose egos outweighed the earth.

Hilda was more than glad to return to Florida after Gloria's successful, sold out tour. When Gloria's concert manager visited them in Orlando and he went over the receipts from the concert, Gloria was astounded.

She immediately said, "Well, I will be taking off the next five years, except just for occasional appearances." She handed her manager, Jasper, a check and said, "This should hold you until I feel in the mood for traveling. It will come and then I will contact you. I want to live a normal life for awhile and do just what I want to do when I want to do it. You have been a very good manager or else we would not have made so much money."

Hilda observed Gloria as she handled the transaction with her concert manager and felt that she knew what she was doing. He left in good spirits, asking Gloria to contact him when she was ready. No more worries relative to business, after all, she was a wealthy young lady so let her do what she wants to do.

Feeling so alive, Hilda told Gloria that she might go into New York for the week-end and see Regis in his new play on Broadway. Gloria thought that would be a good idea and said that she would like to come along to check upon a couple of her concert friends.

They had a great time in the big city and on their way back, Hilda asked Gloria to make a stop over in Jackson, Mississippi and visit her home in D'Lo before returning to Orlando. She seemed very anxious to see Hilda's old home.

Hilda called Jerlene and asked her to meet them at the airport. Jerlene giggled over the phone as Hilda told her that she would have someone with her and to make sure everything was looking good.

Jerlene said, "Miss Hilda, you know I keep everything looking good just as if you were here everyday. It will be so good to see you, even if for just a day or two. Don't worry, I will be at the airport on time, anyway, I love driving that new car you left me. I am going to fix up a big meal and have some drinks cooling for us all when you get here. I can hardly wait." As Hilda slowly hung up the phone, she could hear Jerlene giggling in the background.

Coming into the Jackson Airport, Hilda said."Gloria, Jerlene will meet us and look after everything, as you know she has been my personal maid, housekeeper for years. She loves to drive my car that I left for her to use. So we don't have anything to worry about when we get on the ground."

As Hilda and Gloria approached the entrance to the passenger terminal, Hilda looked up and she saw Jerlene waving and screaming, "Over here, over here, Miss Hilda." She noticed that Jerlene had really dressed herself up for this occasion. Looking better than I have ever seen her, thought Hilda as she hugged her neck.

Hilda looked at Gloria's stunned expression as she said, "Gloria, this is Jerlene, my good friend."

Gloria gave Jerlene a slight hug, saying, "I am so delighted to meet you after hearing Miss Hilda talk about you so much."

"Well, I hope all the talk was good anyway," giggled Jerlene. "We have been together for so many years, she seems like a sister instead of my employer. We have had lots of happy times together and I am very grateful."

As Hilda and Gloria waited for their pieces of luggage, Jerlene went to move her car into the front of the terminal so the porter could load it. Surprisingly, it didn't take very long and they were on their way to D'Lo.

Jerlene was in control of most of the conversation on the way down from Jackson. She told them that she had everything planned out while they were visiting Webber House.

"I have drinks being cooled when we arrive and want you all to relax and enjoy," said Jerlene. "I have prepared an excellent country meal which was always a favorite of Miss Hilda's."

Hilda kept a close watch on Gloria's body language and her facial expressions when looking at Jerlene. I know that it wasn't caused by her being a black woman with beautiful bronze skin. Her adopted parents were black with skin much like Jerlene's.

Hilda thought, what a scandal and much gossip there would be if the people in D'Lo had an inkling of what the situation was in her household. Some would probably ask her to move out for good and make it very difficult for Jerlene to remain in D'Lo. She was sure that the secrets had been sealed long ago and the black folks were not going to tell on Jerlene having babies by Poppa.

Arriving at Webber House in D'Lo, Jerlene got out of the car and ran inside, asking them to come on in. Hilda put her arm around Gloria as they walked upon the huge veranda.

To Hilda this was a dream come true, Gloria being at home in D'Lo. Arm in arm they walked around the veranda and then into the house as Hilda wanted her daughter to see her home.

Gloria said, "Mother, I know you must have loved living here. It is such a peaceful, relaxing place. I know that I would have loved being here as a young child."

Hilda hugged her saying, "I need to go to the bathroom."

Before she could open the door to the bathroom, her eyes were overflowing with tears. She didn't want to break down in front of Gloria.

When Hilda returned from the bathroom, she found Gloria out in the kitchen with Jerlene. She was answering questions put forth from Gloria about the house and yards. Gloria had fallen in love with Webber House. Jerlene set up drinks at a table on the back veranda. She even had Hilda's old chinese lantern glowing with a soft light as the evening had become hazy with first touch of night.

Gloria commented, "Now this is very romantic. I could enjoy lots of these evenings. Listen to the crickets as Jerlene calls them. They must be calling for each other."

The next day Gloria said the situation at the Webber House was great for resting and persuaded Hilda to stay for a week. Of course, this was what the doctor ordered as far as Hilda was concerned. They lolled around sunbathing and Jerlene fed them well every day. Hilda, Gloria and Jerlene went several times into Jackson shopping like three teen age girls. Of course, Gloria was glad that she was not bothered with anyone asking for autographs like they do up East and other places. Only one person in D'Lo had asked or inquired who was the young lady visiting in D'Lo. Hilda answered her by saying, "It is just a friend from Connecticut."

The day before Gloria decided that she wanted to return to her house in Orlando, Hilda had a premonition that some day soon she would be back in D'Lo for good.

She let Jerlene know that she would have to take them to the airport in Jackson. Gloria was anxious to be on the move again.

Back in Florida, Gloria was busy practicing for local concerts in the New York area, plus a recall back to Carnegie Hall. She really didn't need to work because she had plenty of money plus all the real estate that had been left by the Langleys. It was in the process of being liquidated into cash as she had turned it over to a realtor but she loved her music. She would go away for a few weeks at a time but would always come back to her home in Orlando. She was a very independent lady and ruled her career with the same manager that started her on her way.

It seems this went on for several years until Hilda felt that she needed to take a vacation in D'Lo. Gloria didn't want to accompany her, so she left for D'Lo in a brand new Lincoln that she purchased with some of Poppa's money. She felt eerie about being out on the road alone but in her mind she had been alone for years. Of course, she had Gloria who was busy with her career and slowly getting ready to retire.

Hilda took inventory, while driving into Mississippi from Florida, thinking that she was getting too old for all this moving around, maybe she should just come back to Webber House and enjoy.

It had been several weeks since she had heard from Jerlene and she hadn't contacted her that she was driving in from Florida. Hilda thought she would be one surprised woman, especially after she told her that she would be around for awhile.

On the coast, near Gulfport, Mississippi, Hilda stopped to call Jerlene but she couldn't get her on the telephone. She made another attempt in Hattiesburg but still no answer. Hilda became worried so she hurried on to D'Lo.

Arriving at Webber house, she felt that something had happened because it was dusk dark and no lights anywhere. She remembered that Jerlene always had lights on everywhere in the house when evening shadows began to fall. Also, after getting out of the car, looking around the yard and house, everything looked unkept.

She found her key under the stone by the front steps and opening the door to go inside, she realized that no one was here. Jerlene had been found dead in her bed after some people from Chalmette had visited her one week end.

Hilda waking from a bad dream, knew she was finally at home when she heard her friend, Ila chatting away as usual as she entered the front yard.

BVG